Seven Grandmothers

Also by Reba Paeff Mirsky

THIRTY-ONE BROTHERS AND SISTERS
(Winner of the 1952 Charles W. Follett Award)

Grandmothers

by Reba Paeff Mirsky

Illustrated by W. T. Mars

Follett Publishing Company

CHICAGO

NEW YORK

Also by Reba Paeff Mirsky

THIRTY-ONE BROTHERS AND SISTERS
(Winner of the 1952 Charles W. Follett Award)

NOMUSA AND THE NEW MAGIC

Follett Publishing Company
1010 West Washington Boulevard
Chicago, Illinois 60607

LIBRARY OF CONGRESS CATALOG CARD NUMBER: 55-7502

SIXTH PRINTING

T/L 7840

TO MY HUSBAND AND SIBUSISIWE

Seven Grandmothers

Chapter 1

"Look, Nomusa!" whispered Themba. "Who is *that?*"

Nomusa looked up quickly. A strange woman had entered the kraal, a most extraordinary-looking woman, wearing crossed strips of brown and white goatskin over her chest and necklaces and fringes of many-colored beads around her wrinkled neck.

"She must be an *inyanga* from the way she is dressed," Nomusa said in a low voice.

She walked respectfully toward the witch doctor, followed by her little brother, Themba. He could not keep his eyes off the five dried gall bladders and the striped feathers in the stranger's straggly reddened hair and the tuft of black fur that stuck out from the back of her head like a bushy tail.

Both children knelt before the woman with bowed heads, to show their respect for an elder. They did not speak until the witch doctor spoke to them; it would not have been polite.

"*Sakubona,*" the witch doctor said to Nomusa. "I see you, my child."

"I see you, too, *inkosikazi,*" Nomusa replied, her eyes still downcast. It was not polite to look directly at an older person, either.

But even without looking directly at the witch doctor, Nomusa and Themba could see that her whole head was greased and covered with a red clay, and that in the middle of her forehead a coin dangled from a thin braid. An oxhide skirt hung to her ankles, around which she wore bands of twisted copper and beads. Above these were other anklets of dried cocoons and pods containing seeds or pebbles, which rattled as the *inyanga* moved. A wide beaded belt encircled her waist, and bead pendants hung from her ears, joined together by a double bead string tied under her chin.

In her left hand she held a small black and white oxhide shield; in her right, she carried a beaded wand-stick at the end of which the white tail of a gnu was attached.

"Where is Chief Zitu?" asked the witch doctor. "I have been sent for."

"He is in the hut of Big Mother, our *Ugogo*," answered Nomusa. "I shall take you to him, *inkosikazi*." That was the respectful way to address an important person if it was a woman; if it was a man, he was called *inkosi.*

Nomusa rose to lead the way, carrying her pet, Dube, the little striped monkey. Small brothers and sisters appeared as the word went about that an *inyanga* was in their kraal. Excited but cautious, they remained a short distance behind the witch doctor, drawing nearer and nearer in order to get a good look at her.

Nomusa and Themba, followed by their small sisters and brothers of various ages and sizes, squeezed behind the witch doctor as she entered.

She saluted Zitu with *"Bayete!"* and bowed low, for he was a chief.

Raising his right arm, Zitu replied, *"Sakubona."*

The children arranged themselves quietly against the wall of the women's side of the hut. Soon Zitu's six wives, their hair reddened and greased, appeared in the crowded hut. Learning of the *inyanga's* arrival they had hurried back from hoeing their vegetable gardens, some with babies slung in goatskins on their backs.

Zitu sat apart, to the right of the hearth, the men's side. Ugogo lay on her straw sleeping mat covered with a soft kaross, a blanket. It was made of smooth goatskins stitched together.

The *inyanga's* piercing eyes darted about the hut, inspecting it. So far she had not even glanced at Ugogo. Suddenly her eyes widened and she exclaimed, "Someone here is sick!" and waved her beaded wand-stick menacingly.

Startled, Nomusa and the other children flattened themselves closer to the wall.

"What's she doing?" whispered Themba, worried.

"I don't know yet," replied Nomusa softly.

When *Ugogo* coughed, Nomusa's mother, Makanya, moved quickly to her side.

"Sister, give me the water gourd," she said to one

of Zitu's other wives. *Ugogo* drank thirstily.

When *Ugogo* finished drinking, the *inyanga* began to leap about. The striped feathers, the dried gall bladders and the fur tuft bobbed in her hair; the coin swung dizzily over her forehead. With birdlike movements she turned her head here, there, seeking something. Suddenly she proclaimed, *"Yo,* Chief Zitu's mother is sick!"

At this discovery, Nomusa exchanged amused glances with her half-sisters, Sisiwe and Hlamba.

"We'll soon find out who or what has caused her sickness," declared the witch doctor. "Bring me a brown-spotted goat right away."

Zitu called to Nomusa, "Go, my daughter, and fetch it. There is one tied outside the fence of the cattle enclosure. Hurry!"

"Very well, *Ubaba,* I go."

$\mathcal{L}$EAVING DUBE with Themba, Nomusa
pushed her way through the sisters and
brothers. She ran lest she miss too much of
the *inyanga's* treatment of her grandmother. Nomusa
had been impressed by the witch doctor's interesting,
intelligent face; she thought she looked exceedingly
clever. She had to be clever to be able to find lost articles

and cure sicknesses with magic and special herbs!

But Nomusa had doubts, too. Perhaps the *inyanga* tried to make people think she was cleverer than she really was. These thoughts made Nomusa feel guilty, even a little fearful. If the *inyanga* knew!

Nomusa was sad to part with one of their little goats. She tried to stifle her misgivings, worried now that she might hinder Big Mother's recovery by her doubting.

The little goat was tied outside the cattle enclosure fence, just as Zitu had said. Nomusa knew that if it had been inside, her father would have sent one of the boys; it was considered bad luck for the animals if a girl entered the enclosure.

Nomusa led the brown-spotted goat to *Ugogo's* hut, but at the entrance the goat stubbornly pulled back as if it sensed danger. Vainly Nomusa tugged and pulled. Finally, in desperation she got behind the animal and shoved with all her might. This worked, and the frightened goat rushed headlong into the hut.

Smelling the food cooking, he leaped toward the cook pot. Just in time, Themba grabbed the goat's stubby tail to keep him from upsetting the pot and scattering the burning embers. The straw-thatched hut could easily have caught fire.

Nomusa smiled at her little brother approvingly for preventing a bad accident.

Into half-gourds the *inyanga* poured powdered herbs from the oxhorns hanging from her beaded belt. Into them she stirred water, whereupon some medicines became white, some black.

Roughly she dragged the goat toward *Ugogo,* but the frightened little animal bleated and pulled away; the witch doctor became gentler, smoothing down the goat's disheveled forelock, patting him reassuringly. This seemed to overcome his distrust, and he became quiet.

With the midday sun high, the older brothers and half-brothers, who were the herdboys, began returning from the fields with the cattle belonging to their father and mothers.

The boys were shouting at the cattle to keep them from straying while being led into the cattlefold. There was the usual joking and laughing among them as they chased and prodded the cows into line.

Hearing the commotion outside, Zitu said to Nomusa, "My daughter, tell your brothers to be quiet. Remind them there is sickness here."

Again Nomusa shoved her way out of the hut.

"*Tula!*" she called to the herdboys. "Hush! *Ugogo* is very sick, and a witch doctor is here. *Ubaba* sent me to tell you."

Hearing this, all the brothers clustered round Nomusa. Her half-brother Dinga said, "An *inyanga* right here in our kraal? Let's hurry so we can see what she looks like and what she does!"

By prodding and pushing, the boys finally succeeded in getting the cattle into the enclosure. Immediately, the younger brothers tied the cows' front legs to keep them from moving during the milking.

For a few moments Nomusa stood watching them take down the wooden buckets from the pegs inside the cattlefold, a special one for each mother. The younger boys led the calves to nurse from the cows; as soon as the milk began to flow, they were driven away, and the older boys commenced the milking.

It seemed to Nomusa that today they were speedier than usual in their haste to see the witch doctor. She ran back to her grandmother while the brothers hurried with their full milk pails to their mothers' huts; soon the fourteen of them joined Nomusa.

Silently they walked to the men's side of the hut, kneeling respectfully before their father.

The witch doctor was chanting, accompanied by the rhythmic clapping of all, even the smallest child. Suddenly, she broke into a wild dance; her medicine horns, the snuff gourd and spoon, the bead necklaces and fringes, swung crazily. She rushed toward *Ugogo,* then away from her, waving the wand-stick threateningly, as if pursuing a fierce enemy.

Stamping her feet, she thrust her gnu-tail wand before her and brandished the oxhide shield; then, unexpectedly, she whirled in dizzy circles until Nomusa thought she would surely fall and hurt herself.

The *inyanga's* dancing stopped abruptly; she stood still and cocked her head, listening to something. All at once she jumped back and dashed toward the startled children. She commanded everyone to clap harder; as they did so, she called upon Zitu's ancestral spirits.

"*Idlozi,* why have you sent this sickness to our great

chief's mother? Who has offended you, and how?'' cried the *inyanga* loudly.

Jerking spasms seized her body; now she stamped so vigorously that swirls of ashes from the hearth rose up in a thick cloud.

"The *inyanga* must be cold," observed Themba. "See how she is shivering."

The hut was in an uproar with the sound of clapping, stamping, shouting, chanting. Even Dube added his chattering to the confusion. Poor *Ugogo!* thought Nomusa, how uncomfortable she must be with all this noise and the stifling air! She saw her grandmother withdraw under her kaross as if to escape from the uproar and pressure of so many people around her. Her patient face was lined with pain.

The witch doctor stopped dancing. Swiftly she bent down, putting her ear to the floor, motioning excitedly for everyone to be still.

She listened intently, then sprang up quickly as if struck.

"Look out! The *idlozi* are speaking. They're angry. They say proper sacrifices have not been made for a long time. The chief's mother is sick to remind you of your duty. Hurry and bring a red hen, then the chief's mother will sleep and get well."

With a piercing yell she tore a seedpod anklet from her leg and handed it to Nomusa's mother. Makanya

sprang up from beside her mother-in-law to carry out
the command.

Nomusa noticed her father relax. Now that the
witch doctor knew the reason for his mother's sickness,
they could do something about it and *Ugogo* would get
well.

Everyone followed the *inyanga's* gaze upward into
the thatch of the ceiling. Suddenly voices, mumbled
words, could be heard; then whole sentences were uttered
explosively as they descended downward, the clicks in
the Zulu language sounding like the rapid popping of
corks.

Watching, Nomusa discovered to her surprise that
the witch doctor's throat was moving, though her lips
were not.

"By dog, the woman knows how to throw her voice
up to the roof," thought Nomusa, but she resolved not
to say anything about it.

The ancestral spirits continued, "The goat need not
be sacrificed now; the offense to us has not been too
great. The hen will be sufficient. Let *Ugogo* eat part of
it and set aside the rest for us. Don't forget or neglect

to honor your ancestors lest sickness and bad luck beset you."

Nomusa and Themba grinned in relief. The little goat would be spared! Just then their mother entered with the hen fluttering under her bare arm; she offered it to the *inyanga* who accepted it the polite way, with hands outstretched, palms held upward.

"I give you thanks," she said.

The talking from the roof stopped; the witch doctor knelt beside *Ugogo*. Taking a knife from her belt she made a slit in the hen's breast, letting the blood drip into a half-gourd. She poured into it some powdered herbs, whipping it up until a fine white foam formed on the mixture.

"*Yo,* it's white medicine," Nomusa told Sisiwe softly. "It's a good sign."

She watched the witch doctor smear the foam over *Ugogo's* forehead while she chanted a happy song she had made up.

Then she turned to Zitu and said, "Your mother will surely recover if someone can find a cream-colored snake within the kraal."

The words were hardly out of her mouth when there slithered through the hut entrance just such a snake.

"*Awu!*" gasped Themba, clutching Nomusa and jumping back. "There it is!"

Chapter 3

THE AMAZED children huddled together watching the snake glide to the end of the hut and climb the wall to the roof top. Burrowing through the thick thatch, it soon disappeared, flipping its tail as if waving good-by.

A heavy silence fell upon everyone; all eyes turned to the witch doctor. Triumphantly she clapped her

hands and shouted, "It's a good omen! One of Chief
Zitu's ancestors has returned in the form of a snake to
show they are no longer displeased."

Just as she finished saying this, *Ugogo* sneezed explosively.

"Good luck!" exclaimed Zitu, smiling.

This helped to ease the mounting tension in the
hut, and the children began to titter a little. When they
saw their father laugh, and their six mothers, too, they
let loose in uncontrolled giggles.

Now Zitu raised his hand, and the hut became quiet
again.

"I remember something," he said. "When the beer
was made for the last feast, we forgot to pour some on
the ground for our *idlozi*. We must never forget our
ancestors, never! Some day I shall become an ancestor,
and I should be greatly displeased if you did not respect
and remember me properly."

The children nodded their heads, promising never
to neglect his spirit.

The witch doctor now helped *Ugogo* sit up. All
the mothers gathered round, eager to do something for

her, offering her mealie porridge or mashed pumpkin or water.

Makanya pointed to the hut entrance, indicating that the children should leave. Nomusa was the first to start and was followed by the others. Suddenly she turned back with Themba.

"I forgot to take the goat back," she told her father and put her hand on the animal's forelock to lead it out.

"No, my daughter, leave it here," he said. "If the *inyanga* has cured *Ugogo,* the goat will be her payment. Tomorrow you and Themba may take it to her kraal."

Nomusa and Themba could not hide their disappointment. They went out again and saw the hungry children dashing to their own mothers' hut; it was already long past eating time. Nomusa and Themba followed their brothers to their own hut.

Mdingi, Kangata and Themba pushed each other roughly trying to reach the vine hammock that held their eating mats.

All at once Nomusa heard her mother exclaim, "Where is Bala?"

"Bala?" repeated Nomusa.

Everyone stared at Bala's empty sleeping mat.

"*Yo, Umama,* but I left her there fast asleep when Themba and I were outside making the thread for our beads," declared Nomusa.

Themba looked under Bala's mat as if he might find his little sister there. "She's not here," he announced gaily. "She's hiding somewhere; playing a trick on us."

Mdingi ran to peer behind the large grain baskets standing against the back wall; Kangata searched around the tall water jars and beer calabashes expecting Bala to spring out and surprise them.

Nomusa's mother said, "Bala was in your care, Nomusa. Why did you leave her unattended? Your father will be very angry to hear of this."

"It was because of the *inyanga's* arrival," Nomusa said, ashamed. "When she entered the kraal, Themba and I took her to *Ugogo's* hut."

"Then we forgot all about Bala, didn't we, Nomusa?" said Themba unhelpfully.

"Perhaps Bala has wandered out of the kraal into the veld and met a leopard," suggested Kangata.

Nomusa's eyes grew larger with terror at the idea.

Frantically she looked again behind anything tall enough to hide her little sister. She even pulled down the goat-skin and oxhide karosses hanging from a vine rope against the wall.

"We must look everywhere in the kraal now," said Makanya. "She may have wandered into one of the other huts looking for us when we were with *Ugogo*."

Themba, overcome with hunger, bent over the cook pot and reached for a piece of pumpkin.

"No, no, Themba," said his mother. "We must all wait until we find Bala."

Ruefully Themba licked the tips of his fingers. He and his brothers looked longingly at the food which gave off such a tantalizing aroma. Bala's disappearance was a nuisance, and Themba could not take it seriously.

The whole family left the hut, Makanya first, Themba last. The strong sunshine was dazzling after the dimness of the hut. Nomusa raised her hand to shade her eyes, looking in all directions for Bala.

By now no one but themselves was outdoors. Zitu's five other wives and their children were in their huts eating. Nomusa wondered if her father was in his own

hut or with Magalana, one of the other mothers, whose
turn it was for his visit.

"*Yo,* how angry he will be if we don't find Bala
right away," Nomusa thought. Surely she must have

been bewitched to have forgotten about her little sister so completely.

Mdingi and Kangata left to search the grain bins in the cattle enclosure as well as in the small animal pens and the chicken coops. Nomusa could hear them calling urgently, "Bala! Bala!"

Makanya told Nomusa, "We must go to each hut and inquire about her. And we must hurry; clouds are gathering, so it is wooing rain."

First they entered Sisiwe's hut, the one nearest their own. With her younger brothers and sisters she was sitting on a large mat to the left of the hearth, the older brothers to the right. Her mother was pouring water from an earthenware jug onto the outstretched hands of her children, holding a basin underneath to catch the drip.

The children rubbed their hands briskly, then shook them dry.

"*Sakubona*," greeted Sisiwe's mother. "We would be happy if you would stay and eat with us. We have much food today; the soft rains have been good for our vegetable garden. Sisiwe, fetch mats for them."

"Thank you, my sister," said Makanya, "but we have come to inquire about Bala. We do not know where she is."

Sisiwe and her mother exchanged surprised glances; they shook their heads. "No, alas, we have not seen her."

"Excuse us for troubling you and stay well," said Makanya. She and Nomusa left to look elsewhere.

Outside Makanya said, "While I go to Zizile's hut, you go to Magalana's."

Nomusa ran across the kraal yard to the furthest hut which belonged to her father's youngest wife. The mounting worry made her head ache. Perhaps her father would be there!

She stooped under the low opening and bumped into Puleng, her dog.

Nomusa bowed to Magalana, "I see you."

"I see you, too," answered Magalana cordially.

Nomusa was thankful to see that her father was not there. Magalana sat with her baby at her breast. The other children were eating warm white potatoes. When one of the children picked up a potato from his eating mat with his left hand, his mother smacked it lightly, warning, "Not with the left hand, Shagana; use the right, always, otherwise it will bring bad luck."

"Try some of our potatoes, Nomusa. They are especially good today," said Magalana.

"Thank you, our mother, but I have come to ask if Bala has been here to play with Punga. We do not know where she is."

"She has not been here. Was there no one to look after her?"

Nomusa blushed and said, "I fear there was not, our mother. Then I shall go to search elsewhere."

"Go well, and look carefully — everywhere," urged Magalana.

Nomusa came out of the hut in time to see her mother leaving Zizile's hut. She wore the same worried expression as before, so Nomusa knew she too, had been unsuccessful.

Makanya glanced in the direction of the other two huts they had not yet visited. They were the last of the six belonging to Zitu's wives, one belonging to Hlamba's mother, the other to Zabala's.

Makanya pointed to Hlamba's hut and said, "Go

quickly, Nomusa, and inquire; I'll go to Zabala's. If Bala is not in one of these, I don't know what we shall do!"

"Yes, *Umama*," said Nomusa, utterly miserable; to herself she murmured, "It's all my fault."

Nomusa entered Hlamba's hut; they had just finished eating. Hlamba's face brightened when she beheld Nomusa.

"Welcome, welcome, Nomusa. See who is here! Khotiza has just returned from Sigazi's kraal," she said proudly.

Khotiza was Hlamba's eldest sister; she would be married to Sigazi as soon as the bride-dowry was decided upon. Everyone in the kraal knew about the stiff bargaining that was taking place between Zitu and Sigazi's father. It was a matter of whether ten or twelve cows would be given in exchange for Khotiza.

"Sit down, Nomusa," urged Khotiza. "Help us with the beadwork if you have time. We have so much to do to get ready for the wedding. I have already begun composing my bridal song and dances. And I have chosen you, my sister, to be in my bridal party."

Nomusa said, "I thank you for the honor and I would gladly stay to help you, but I have come to ask if you have seen Bala. She disappeared from our hut when the witch doctor arrived, and we do not know where she is."

"Perhaps she is in one of the other huts with Punga," suggested Hlamba. "She has not been here."

"She is not with him, either. I'll go see if our

mother has found her at Zabala's hut. It is the last place in the kraal we can try. As soon as I find Bala, I'll come to help you, Khotiza. Remain in peace."

Not one of the other mothers, sisters or brothers had reproached her for her neglect, and Nomusa was grateful.

A terrible thought now entered her head. What if Bala was not in Zabala's hut either! Her heart raced faster with worry. She waited outside Zabala's hut for her mother. When she did not come out right away Nomusa's hopes rose. Perhaps she had found Bala there and was now having a pleasant visit.

Nomusa's thoughts were interrupted by her mother asking, "Was Bala in Hlamba's hut?" and she realized Bala had not been found; and now there were no other huts to go to.

Zabala, who would be chief when his father died, accompanied Makanya. Turning to Nomusa he said, "You must go to our father and tell him about Bala; then he will call out a searching party. It must be done before the sun sets, for once it is dark there will be great danger to our little sister. Only yesterday we saw a leopard stalking one of our calves, and he may still be lurking about. Let us go to *Ubaba's* hut right away."

Zitu's hut faced the entrance of the kraal. They found the entrance to it barred by a reed door to show he was not at home.

"Let us see if *Ubaba* is still with *Ugogo*," suggested Zabala.

This was the moment Nomusa dreaded. She was sure he would punish her severely. Perhaps he would forbid her to be in Khotiza's bridal party or be present at the feast for Mdingi and the other boys after the ear-piercing ceremony.

In front of *Ugogo's* hut, Makanya told Nomusa, "Go in and tell your father about Bala. Zabala and I will wait here."

Nomusa's eyes grew moist at the prospect before her. Hastily she wiped away a tear with the back of her hand.

"I go, *Umama*," said Nomusa softly, as if walking to her doom.

Chapter 4

THE INYANGA was sitting beside *Ugogo,*
    chatting with her like an old friend, when
    Nomusa entered the hut. Zitu sat across
from them serenely smoking his ox-horn pipe.

Nomusa stood silent until they took notice of her.

"Hau! I see my daughter, the brave hunter," teased
Zitu.

"*Bayete, Ubaba.* I have come with bad news," said Nomusa. "We cannot find Bala. We have searched everywhere within the kraal, and no one has seen her. When I took the *inyanga* to *Ugogo* I left Bala asleep in the hut, then forgot about her. I deserve whatever punishment you give me," said Nomusa bowing her head.

"*Awu!* This is very bad," said Zitu, laying down his pipe. Nomusa was surprised at his unexpected calmness.

The witch doctor turned to Nomusa and studied her face. In a corner the goat was tied up with the baby calf, nibbling cornhusks which rustled as he ate and tossed them about.

Nomusa felt the long silence unendurable; sorrowfully she knelt beside *Ugogo,* waiting for the blow to fall. *Ugogo* took Nomusa's hand and stroked it affectionately to comfort her. Nomusa's shoulders were stooped, her face clouded with fear; she was a pathetic little figure.

Zitu broke the silence at last.

"This is the first time you have failed in a task, my daughter, and I confess I am disappointed. Before I appoint a searching party, we should ask the *inyanga* to help us. She is an expert at finding things."

Nomusa turned to the *inyanga* appealingly. The witch doctor looked into her sad face, put her arm tenderly on her shoulder and told Zitu, *"Inkosi,* I believe this daughter, Nomusa, would make an excellent *inyanga*. Do you dream much, my child?"

"Sometimes," murmured Nomusa, wondering what this had to do with helping her find Bala.

"Well, if you dream a lot, it is a good sign. It means you can be in close communication with the spirits of your ancestors. When you are a little older you should come to my school for witch doctors. I will teach you how to cure people, find lost articles, get rid of enemies and other useful things. I could even tell you how to make a young man fall in love with you," and the witch doctor chuckled. "When you bring me the goat I'll show you what we do at my school. Will you come?"

Her head turned away politely, Nomusa said, "Yes, *inkosikazi,* if my father says I may."

Zitu turned to the *inyanga* and said, "Since my daughter is so careless as to lose a small sister, it would be a very good idea if she learned how to find lost things." He picked up his pipe trying to suppress a smile.

"*Hawu!*" exclaimed the witch doctor. "I have an itchy feeling in my shoulders! The *idlozi* wish to speak to me. I must take some snuff quickly."

The witch doctor shook some snuff out of her ox-horn into a small ivory spoon and shoveled it into her wide nostrils. She waited, poised, and sneezed so violently that her whole body shook. She announced excitedly, "Bala is in this hut!"

Ugogo smiled and patted Nomusa's moist hand reassuringly.

Zitu asked his mother, "Have you seen Bala, *Umama?*"

"That I have, my son," she replied cheerfully.

Nomusa stared at her grandmother in amazement.

"Oh, *where,* dear *Ugogo!*" she begged.

"Come closer, my child," she beckoned, and slowly lifted one corner of her kaross.

Lying underneath it was Bala, fast asleep, contentedly sucking a plump finger. On her face was such a blissful expression that everyone burst out laughing.

"Bala!" exclaimed Nomusa, touching her to make sure.

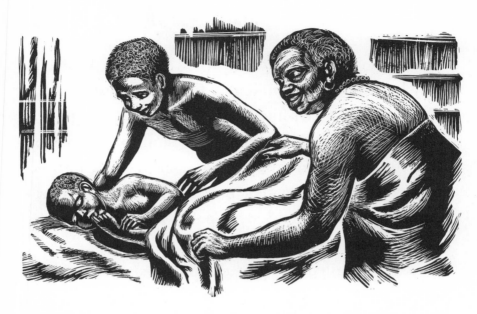

Bala awoke murmuring, "I want my *Ugogo* to tell me the Dassie story again. I like it."

Ugogo said, "I think you were sleeping when I told it to you. If you listened, show me, and tell it to No-musa."

In a piping voice, Bala droned, "Once upon a time, when the king of the animals was giving out tails to all the other animals in the forest, he called them to come to a certain place to get their tails. But Dassie, the rock rabbit, was lazy and didn't want to come out of his hole because it was raining. So, when the other animals ran by his hole to get their tails, he asked them, 'Get a tail for me, will you? I don't want to go out in the rain and get wet.'

"But because Dassie didn't go himself he didn't get a tail, and no one bothered to ask for one for him."

"Well, Bala, and what does the story mean?" asked Zitu.

"It means I mustn't be lazy, *Ubaba,*" said Bala, turning to her grandmother for corroboration.

"Yes, little one. We Zulus say that if you want anything well done, you must do it yourself," *Ugogo* pointed out.

"Very well, Nomusa. Take Bala home now; it's a good thing you found her," said Zitu firmly.

Nomusa swooped up her little sister, hugging her so tightly that Bala screamed, "Let me down, Nomusa; you're squeezing me like a rock python!"

As Nomusa was leaving, Zitu said, "Tomorrow you and Themba will take the brown-spotted goat to the *inyanga's* kraal. Now bring Bala to her mother. No doubt she is worrying about her."

Nomusa hastened outdoors, holding Bala tight. Joyfully, Makanya took Bala from Nomusa and hoisted her onto her back. Zabala asked, "How do you suppose she got to *Ugogo's* hut without anyone seeing her?"

"*I* know," said Bala impishly, "but I won't tell you."

"It was naughty of you," reproved Makanya, but her eyes shone with happiness that Bala was safe.

When Mdingi, Kangata, and Themba saw their mother, Bala, and Nomusa approaching, they ran to them joyfully.

"*Halahala,* hurrah!" shouted Themba. "Now we can have something to eat!"

Mdingi asked Nomusa, "How is *Ugogo?*"

"Oh, she is better. She is telling stories again." Nomusa's face glowed with happiness; her grandmother was better and her little sister was safe.

Chapter 5

By THE TIME Nomusa awoke next morning,
the sun had risen half way over the hills.
Already a pinhole of daylight penetrated
through a chink in the mud wall of the hut.

Nomusa rose quietly and poked some twigs into
the smouldering embers. She blew on them softly
to start up the flame that would heat the cook pot. There

was still some mealie porridge in it, left over from supper the night before.

She decided that today she would sweep around the hut more carefully than usual; she would sweep away yesterday's troubles and bad luck and thus start the day fresh. Bala's disappearance had given her a bad fright.

With Dube perched on her shoulder, Nomusa opened the hut door a crack and slipped through quietly, trying not to waken the others by letting in too much light.

She could hear the female ground hornbill, the *intsingizi,* crying, *"Ngiyamuka, ngiya muka, ngiyamuka, ngiya kwabetu:* I am going, I am going off to my people."

Nomusa laughed to herself as the grumbling answer soon came in an undertone, from the hidden male hornbill, *"Hamba, hamba, kad'usho:* go, go, for goodness' sake! You've been saying so long enough!"

Nomusa knew, of course, that hornbills did not really say such words, but their chatter and scolding were always interpreted by *Ugogo* as meaning that, simply to amuse her delighted grandchildren.

Before long Nomusa caught sight of the female

hornbill. On her bill was a bright yellow protuberance, like a piece of horn, which was surrounded by a scarlet rim. Its tail was long and tapering, the two middle feathers nearly twice the length of the rest of them.

The bird was now near the thorn fence of the kraal, moving by short leaps and hops. Nomusa saw how she picked up some mealie kernels lying on the ground, tossed them into the air, then caught them in her bill, like a juggler, before swallowing them. The bird did it so skillfully, without dropping a single kernel, that Nomusa watched fascinated. Although the hornbill was only a little larger than a field crow, Nomusa had heard that these birds were sometimes able to capture small snakes and devour them.

Nomusa was thinking, I hope this bird doesn't alight on any of our huts or it will be a bad omen. Always one had to be on one's guard against doing the wrong thing, and what a long list of things there was that a girl, in particular, shouldn't do! Nomusa had finished sweeping, and had brushed away the dirt in a large circle. If there had been any bad luck hovering near their hut, she had certainly flung it away to the wind.

The rays of the sun pierced the purple shadows in the thorn trees and tinged the feathery acacias golden yellow. The leafless kaffirbloom trees held on to their red blossoms, like tiny bouquets.

Nomusa felt a surge of joy at the beauty of the day. Even the stunted trees looked more attractive than usual.

She began to wonder about the long walk to the *inyanga's* kraal; it might be too far for Themba. Even with many stops to rest, she calculated she could not reach the witch doctor's hut until the sun was at its highest.

As she was leaving for the stream with her water jar, Themba caught up with her and said, "I'll go with you to fill my water gourd for the journey; I'm also taking my bow and arrows to protect you from ferocious animals on the way."

"There will be streams from which we can drink when we go to the witch doctor," she pointed out, "but I'm going to ask Mdingi to lend me his knobkerry. I might need it."

When Nomusa and Themba returned from the stream, their father said, "Nomusa, it is time for you to take the goat to the *inyanga*. Go now with Themba, but you must leave Dube here. Some wild animals are especially fond of monkey meat."

Nomusa's mother told her, "Be sure to be back before dark."

"Very well, *Umama,* we shall go right away," said Nomusa.

"Wait!" Themba ordered loudly for all to hear. "I must get my bow and arrows first."

His self-importance amused the older boys. Mdingi came over and said, "Take my spear with you, Nomusa, if you wish."

"Thank you, Mdingi, but I would rather have your knobkerry. In the daytime I am not likely to meet any fierce animals, excepting wild dogs and baboons, so a knobkerry is sufficient."

Mdingi came back from the hut with a heavy piece of red wood like a thick cane, with a large smooth knob at one end.

Nomusa and Themba went to *Ugogo's* hut, and at the entrance they called out, *"Bayete, Ugogo.* We are here."

Ugogo replied in a strong voice, *"Za,* come in."

They found her sitting beside the hearth fire with a small grandchild, Mapumulo, in her lap. She was telling him a story while waving a bowl of hot porridge back and forth, chanting, *"Heshe, heshe, heshe, tata okushisayo!* Take away what is hot and bring what is cold."

"We have come for the little goat, *Ugogo,"* said Nomusa.

"Take it, my child. There's a grass rope over there to tie on him."

They attached it loosely around the goat's neck and led him out of the hut, calling, "Good-by, *Ugogo!* Good-by, little Mapumulo."

"Tahtahtah! Here, take some cooked pumpkin to eat on the way. You may grow hungry," said *Ugogo.*

Nomusa came back; she picked up a few pieces of pumpkin and wrapped them in a large pawpaw leaf. She handed the package to Themba and licked off the sweet pumpkin juice from her fingers.

When the goat smelled the pumpkin he pulled back, trying to reach the cook pot. To induce it to come along, Themba pinched off a piece of the pumpkin and held it in front of him and that worked very well indeed.

At last they were on their way. Eagerly they set forth in the direction of Damasi's kraal, for that was the shortest way.

The little goat was not troublesome until they passed fields of mealie corn; then he tugged impatiently, wishing to nibble at the stalks.

Nomusa and Themba took turns leading him, but sometimes it required both of them to hold him when he was determined to graze. Now and then Themba fed him bits of pumpkin to keep him moving.

"I'm beginning to think this pumpkin is for the goat instead of for us. I hope it lasts until we get to the *inyanga's* kraal," said Themba.

"It's not as easy as I thought, to take a goat a long distance," observed Nomusa. "Perhaps we should stop at Damasi's kraal and get some extra food. I fear the pumpkin won't last long at this rate."

Themba felt it was just an excuse to see Damasi, but he said, "That's a good idea, Nomusa. Anyway, I would like to show my bow and arrows to Gudazi and Gwala, his little brothers."

"Goodness, we're not going there for a visit, Themba; still the day is young and we could easily spend a few minutes there."

Because of the twisting path that wound through the hills, it took longer to get to Damasi's kraal than Themba thought. Shortly before they reached his kraal, Nomusa and Themba heard shouting and yelling in the field beyond.

"See, Nomusa, Gudazi and Gwala are playing a game with some other boys. Let's see what it is."

Themba ran through the thick grass that reached to his chest, holding high his bow and arrows.

"*Sakubona, sakubona,* Themba," greeted Gudazi and Gwala, delighted to see him. "Come and play *Wenombiba* with us."

Nomusa watched Themba run up to the eight boys lined up in two parallel rows, four opposite each other. They welcomed Themba with enthusiasm and examined his bow and arrows.

"Come into my line," invited Gwala.

"No, into mine," said Gudazi, "the boys stamp harder here."

At first Themba put down his bow and arrows, but when he saw what the game was, he picked them up again. The boys were stamping the grass as hard as they could with their bare feet. Dancing back and forth, they moved from one spot to another, singing,

> *Wenombiba, big rat,*
> *Webuzi elidala, old rat*
> *Woza nganena, come, come this way.*

They chanted as they stamped. All at once Themba saw bush rats of all sizes leaping out of the long grass trying to escape. The boys hurled their long pointed sticks at them excitedly, shouting with joy when their aim was successful. It was a sport they obviously enjoyed. Themba could hardly wait to use his bow and arrows.

Themba, the youngest and smallest of the boys, was at a disadvantage with his short legs, but his attempt to keep up with them earned the respect of his friends.

Suddenly, a large bush rat, lips turned back to bite, leaped out of the grass and made for Gwala's leg. Quickly Themba drew his bow and let an arrow fly. It caught the rat in the neck and it dropped squealing at Gwala's feet.

"You, Themba!" shouted the boys in admiration of his deadly aim. "What a hunter you will be!"

The goat, frightened, strained at his rope and tried to get away, but Nomusa held him firmly. She saw the boys take the dead bush rat by its long tail and hurl it into a growing pile of rats. Later they would be divided and used for a stew.

Themba was more amazed than anyone that he had succeeded in killing the vicious rat. He was proud when the boys slapped his back. Nomusa beckoned for him to come along, so he asked Gudazi, "Where is Damasi?"

"He has left with the cattle. If you have a message, I'll gladly give it to him," said Gudazi.

Nomusa tried not to show her disappointment. "No, we have no message. But we hoped to get some extra food for our journey from Damasi."

Gudazi ran to his hut and returned with food. As they left the boys, Themba said, "We're on our way to the *inyanga*. The goat is for her because she made our *Ugogo* well. I have come with my sister to protect her from danger."

His success with the bush rat had made him slightly boastful. Nomusa was amused.

The boys went back to their game. As they walked along, they could hear them chanting. Now and then Themba looked back longingly for a glimpse of his friends.

To herself Nomusa hummed, "Big rat, old rat, come, come this way," and she wished that girls were

allowed to play such exciting games. She was sure that
she would have been able to spear and club as many
bush rats as the most skillful boys. She promised herself
that some day she would go out to a field by herself and
practice hard with the knobkerry.

Chapter 6

THE AIR BECAME clear and warm as the
sun rose higher. The countryside was turning from a drab brown to fresh green because of the recent rains. In the fields, Nomusa saw
women and girls preparing ground for the new crops.

"I'm getting thirsty," said Themba. "Now I can
drink the water from my gourd. Will you have some?"

"Not yet, I can wait until we reach the stream," said Nomusa.

They stopped while Themba drank, letting the goat wander into the field to nibble some tufts of grass.

Soon after they set forth again, they caught sight of the stream Nomusa was looking for. It was one of the landmarks Zitu had told her to look for. Good, that meant they were near Sigazi's kraal.

It occurred to Nomusa that they ought to stop in and pay their respects to their future kinsmen.

A small yellow blur flashed by in front of her. Themba saw it, too, and pointed excitedly. "Look, a honey bird!" and he raised his bow.

"Don't hurt it, Themba. It does no harm, and it is hardly big enough for one bite," said Nomusa. "I think it is showing us the way to a wild beehive. See, it's waiting for us to notice and follow it."

"What a strange little song it has," observed Themba.

When the honey bird was sure it was noticed, it flew a short distance further on, sang, and again waited. Nomusa and Themba began to follow it. The bird flew from tree to bush, coaxing them to come along; then it remained perched on an acacia branch, turning its head to the right.

"Is it really showing us where there is some honey?" asked Themba. "Let's keep following it, Nomusa. This is fun."

The bird flew off again, a longer distance away. It hid in the thick foliage of a thorn tree and stayed there.

"Oh, we can't go that far now," said Nomusa. Then, seeing Themba's disappointment, she said, "I'll place a stone here so that when we return we'll remember where it is. The honeycomb of the wild bees must be hidden in that very tree."

She placed a large stone prominently on one side of the path, and with her knobkerry drew an arrow pointing toward the tree into which the honey bird had flown.

Again they set out; Nomusa was determined not to stop again for anything. By the time they reached the stream, Nomusa was as thirsty and hungry as Themba. They cupped the water up in their hands and drank.

Nomusa suggested, "Let's sit against that grassy bank and rest a little and eat our pumpkin."

Leaning contentedly against the sun-drenched slope, Nomusa let go of the goat's rope so he could roam and graze freely. Soon Nomusa and Themba grew drowsy.

They were roused by the sound of angry growling mingled with the little goat's frightened bleats. Nomusa and Themba jumped up and climbed up the grassy bank.

In the field below stood the terrified goat; near it was a wild dog, as big as Puleng, Nomusa's dog. It looked somewhat like a hyena, with a coat of dirty yellow marked with irregular patches of coarse brown hair. His sharp cruel barks filled the children with fear; they knew wild dogs often attacked calves, sheep, and goats, for complaints were often brought to their father.

Nomusa raised her knobkerry, aiming it carefully at the ugly creature, while Themba set an arrow to his bow.

Just as they were about to use their weapons, a honey badger appeared from a hole in the ground, not

far from the helpless, trembling goat. This animal was much smaller than the wild dog and stood low on its short legs. The honey badger seemed to be sizing up the situation; then with a quick spring, it leaped on the wild dog, sinking its teeth and claws into the bully.

Surprised and angry, the wild dog attempted to free himself from the honey badger's grip.

Nomusa rushed to the goat and dragged him to a safe distance. Perhaps, she thought, when the honey badger finished with the wild dog, he would try to get the goat for himself. But she and Themba were much too interested in the struggle to leave.

They saw that the wild dog's teeth were having little effect on the honey badger's tough hide with its stiff and bristling gray hairs. They were happy when the wild dog began to show signs of exhaustion. The honey badger, however, seemed to be enjoying the struggle and was as lively as ever.

When the wild dog tried to slink away the honey badger cut him off; he was not yet finished with the exciting sport. But the honey badger finally grew bored with his reluctant adversary; he let the wild dog retreat bit by bit, then with a rush he chased him away.

Before returning to his hole, the honey badger looked all around him; then he made a dash toward Nomusa and Themba. Quickly they pushed their goat behind them. Nomusa held her knobkerry ready to throw. Themba was frightened, but he prepared his bow and arrow.

Just before the honey badger reached them, he stopped suddenly and began toying with some small stones, rolling them over and over as if they were balls.

Cautiously, Themba rolled a pebble toward him to see what he would do. Immediately, the animal rushed

for it, rolling it back and forth excitedly, the way Puleng did. He looked up at Themba, as if begging him to throw another!

Nomusa and Themba smiled, greatly surprised. This time Nomusa gently threw a stone to the badger. Delighted, he pounced on it, rolling it over and over. This play continued until finally he was tired and lay on his back, wriggling on the ground like a happy puppy.

Nomusa and Themba were no longer worried, and they laughed aloud. Themba said, "See what a friendly animal he is. Let's take him home with us and keep him for a pet."

Nomusa was about to agree, but then she thought of Dube and the possible difficulties of keeping the two pets together; so she said, "I don't know how we could get the honey badger to follow us all the way to the witch doctor's kraal and back to ours. If he follows us, we'll keep him; if not, we'll give up the idea."

This seemed reasonable to Themba and they went on, the badger waddling behind them. Occasionally, Themba tossed him a small stone or pebble to encourage him.

They were constantly looking back to make sure that he was still with them, laughing at his leisurely waddle. Suddenly his waddle became a fierce rush. With a mighty leap he landed in front of them so unexpectedly that Nomusa had to grab Themba's arm to keep him from falling.

For a moment Nomusa was sure the honey badger had decided to attack the goat, and she raised her knobkerry to defend him. But now she could see the reason for the badger's surprising behavior. He had seen a viper in front of Themba, who was just about to step on it.

The honey badger grasped the viper's neck just below the head so its poisonous fangs would not pierce his skin. Wriggling and twisting, the yellow-brown viper tried to free himself and attack the badger.

Nomusa and Themba jumped back, dragging the little goat away. Drawing Themba close to her, Nomusa was thankful her little brother was safe. If it had not been for the honey badger, he would have stepped on the viper.

They watched the fight. Like a clever acrobat, the honey badger always managed to slip through the viper's tight ropelike coils without ever loosening his own hold.

His sharp teeth sank deeper and deeper until the viper's head, little by little, dropped to the ground. As its poison-filled fangs struck the red earth, a dark green fluid oozed out of them.

"Ugh, see that!" exclaimed Themba. "If that poison had gotten into me!"

"Oh, Themba, if anything had happened to you it would have been my fault for not watching more carefully, and I could not have returned to our kraal."

The snake lay inert, but the honey badger would not yet let go. From time to time he gave the viper a vigorous shake to see if it was still alive. At last he released his hold, but stood by, watchful and suspicious.

"I think we can go now, Themba," whispered Nomusa. "Let's hurry."

They left the scene of the struggle, no longer throwing stones to the honey badger but watching the path with every step they took. Only once did Themba look back again.

"Look, Nomusa, our honey badger is going down into a hole over there."

"That's too bad, little brother, but I guess it shows he wasn't meant to be our pet after all. Come, we mustn't stop any more, not even for a visit at Sigazi's kraal."

Nomusa yanked the goat's grass leash to urge him along. Already he had forgotten his fright and was serenely nibbling a weed.

Chapter 7

THERE'S THE *inyanga's* kraal," said Nomusa
as they reached the top of a hill. Although
still some distance away, they could see the
witch doctor, surrounded by a few girls, in front of one
of the huts.

Themba said, "I hope we don't have to leave the
inyanga as soon as we have given her the goat."

"Perhaps she'll invite us to stay and see how she teaches girls to become *inyangas*," said Nomusa hopefully. "I might want to become an *inyanga* myself."

"You!" exclaimed Themba, not knowing whether to be glad or not.

"Yesterday the *inyanga* told *Ugogo* and *Ubaba* she thought I would make a good one," Nomusa said.

"If you become a witch doctor, then I'll become a wizard," declared Themba; "then I'll be able to cure sickness and smell out trouble."

"Well, it depends on the kind of wizard you are. You can be a thumb wizard; the people who are in trouble point with their thumbs at him in a special way to show he has guessed the cause of a difficulty."

"What else?"

"You could be a stick-diviner, using sticks that jump around as if they were alive, when they are asked certain questions."

"Oh, that's the kind of a wizard I'd like to be!"

"Wait, you could also be a bone wizard, using special bones from wild animals to find out the cause of someone's trouble."

"Anything else?" asked Themba.

"Let me see. Oh, yes, you could be a rain doctor. Then you could summon rain when it was needed and also ward off storms." She stopped talking for they had reached the *inyanga's* kraal.

They straightened their beads, brushed off some loose earth clinging to their bodies, and then smoothed down the little goat's rumpled forelock. Shyly they entered the kraal. Nomusa could see that the ground had been neatly swept in wide circles.

The witch doctor was sitting on a large reed mat threaded with colored bits of wool; beside her squatted three young girls, two older than herself, judged Nomusa, and one even older than Khotiza.

They were listening to the *inyanga* tell them something with such great emphasis that the lock of hair with the coin fastened to it, swung wildly over her forehead. She was pointing to little piles of something in front of them.

Nomusa and Themba approached the witch doctor, then kneeled respectfully, waiting for her to notice them and speak first. Although the girls were aware of the visitors, they did not turn their attention from the *inyanga's* animated face until she had finished talking.

At last the *inyanga* turned to Nomusa and Themba.

"*Sakubona! Usaphila!* How are you?"

"*Sakubona, inkosikazi!*" they answered together.

"I see you have brought the goat. Bring him to me."

Nomusa handed her the grass rope, and she drew him to her. This time he did not jump back at her touch when she scratched his neck.

"Themba, take the goat and tie him up at the cattle enclosure fence. You'll find some mealie cobs there for him to eat," the *inyanga* told him.

Themba went and the witch doctor turned to Nomusa, saying, "Sit, my child. What news?"

"*Mamó!* What adventures we have had!" Nomusa burst out.

"No serious trouble, I hope? We would be glad to hear what happened," said the *inyanga*.

She and her students moved over on the large mat to make room for Nomusa, who began telling what had befallen them, with frequent interruptions from Themba.

When Nomusa had finished, Themba bent over and whispered to her, "Don't forget to tell them how I killed the big bush rat with my bow and arrow."

The students tried to hide their amusement in back of their hands. The *inyanga* urged, "Tell us about the bush rat, my child."

With Nomusa's encouraging glance, he began. When he exaggerated a little, Nomusa did not contra-

dict him, but looked away. She loved him too much to
deprive him of the innocent pleasure of being the center
of attention and admiration.

When he had finished, the *inyanga* told the students, "Bring some food and weak beer for our guests.
I'll continue with the lesson while they're eating."

She cocked her head suddenly, listening. "Do you
hear the tree crickets? It means the weather will get
hotter because of the powerful sun today.

"Now, if someone has trouble with his eyes, find
the *isihlosa* plant in the veld. You'll recognize it by
the tiny white flowers growing on the sides of the stalk.
Dry it in the sun, crumble it into a fine powder, mix it
with water and apply it to the ailing eyes."

"We hear you," said the attentive students.

Nomusa and Themba listened as they ate, eager to
learn about the secret cures. They ate slowly, remem-
bering not to eat greedily, lest the witch doctor think
there was a famine in their kraal, and thus disgrace their
father.

Continuing, the *inyanga* said, "For a stomach-ache,
find the small shrub *uhlunguhlunga,* or the *unsoksoko*

bush which grows in damp places. Steep the leaves in water, and give it to the patient to drink."

"We are listening," said the girls.

"Suppose someone calls you because of a broken arm, what would you do, Fudukazi?"

"I would put the broken arm with the hand open into a hole in the ground that is partly filled with soft clay," Fudukazi replied. "Then I'd get somebody to help me raise the injured person little by little; then pull the arm out of the hole with force."

"Just so, but remember that sometimes you can bind a broken arm or leg with dried hide or bark," the witch doctor advised.

"I hear you," said Themba seriously, like a student.

Everyone burst out laughing.

"Well, Nomusa, I think I shall keep Themba here and teach him to be a wizard," said the *inyanga* jokingly.

Themba looked worried until Nomusa smiled at him reassuringly.

"Now," the *inyanga* went on, "I'll tell you what to do for skin diseases. Make a paste of the nightshade plant, or use the milky juice of the euphorbia tree, and rub it well on the ailing part."

"Today," said one of the students, "I found some good reeds through which to pour medicines into noses, eyes and ears."

"Good!" commended the *inyanga;* then she pointed to a pile of medicine on the mat. "This is excellent for headache or ear trouble, but for nose bleed use the *utatwe.*"

She looked around to make sure the students were paying attention. One of them passed her the beer calabash from which she drank; then she wiped the edge of the calabash with her hand and passed it to the oldest girl who then passed it to the next oldest girl, until it finally reached Themba.

When he finished drinking, he smacked his lips and said, "When I'm a man, I shall drink strong beer; this beer is only for women and girls."

"Hush! That's impolite, Themba," scolded Nomusa.

The *inyanga* rose and said, "Now I must go to the goat."

Themba bent over and whispered to Nomusa, "She isn't going to hurt our little goat, is she?"

"I hope not," said Nomusa anxiously. "But it's hers now, and she can do with it whatever she wishes."

As soon as the *inyanga* was out of sight, the students turned to Nomusa and Themba, friendly and inquisitive. "Where is your navel cord?" asked one, wishing to know where they came from.

"Are you going to be an *inyanga*, too?" another asked Nomusa.

"Do you dream a lot at night?" asked the third, Makosana. "Because if you do, the ancestral spirits want you to become an *inyanga;* then they can tell you their wishes."

"Oh, how many dreams I have about wild beasts and snakes," said a student. "I hear voices calling me, and sometimes the spirits tell me to leap over bushes or bellow like an ox."

Themba looked at the student-*inyanga* as if she were a little crazy. Guessing his thoughts, she said, "Some people said I was crazy, but soon they saw by certain signs that it was because the *idlozi* were telling me things."

"What were the signs?" inquired Nomusa, curious.

"First of all, I yawned and sneezed a great deal, and I could feel the spirits in my shoulders. Oh, how they itched!"

"My signs were different," said Makosana. "I'd wake up in the middle of the night and begin singing loudly. The ancestors made me compose songs; then I'd order everyone in the kraal to get up and beat time to my music. Soon my family saw I was possessed by a spirit and that either I would have to become an *inyanga* or they would have to call a witch doctor to get rid of the spirit."

"We are listening," said Nomusa and Themba, fascinated.

The girl continued, "My parents decided to call a witch doctor to shut out the spirit that was troubling me. She ground some black medicine and put it into water which I drank."

Themba giggled and caught the reproving glances from the other listeners.

"But nothing helped, so it was decided I had to become an *inyanga*."

The *inyanga* returned with a small bowl of blood.
"*Awu!* Whose blood is that?" demanded Themba.

"Don't worry, my child. I have taken a little of the goat's blood to use in some medicine I am making, but he is as lively as ever," she told him.

Suddenly, Makosana, her eyes half-closed, rose from the mat and began to dance. The *inyanga* and the two students began clapping.

"Clap, my children," ordered the *inyanga*, turning to Nomusa and Themba, who watched eagerly. "It helps her and also coaxes the spirits to stay. She is singing and dancing to a tune they are putting into her."

Nomusa and Themba got out of Makosana's way, for as she danced she hit and bumped against anyone or anything nearby. Her movements were graceful as she waved her arms, turning her head expressively.

Wondering how long this might go on, Nomusa looked up into the sky to see how far the sun had moved. The witch doctor noticed her upward glance and said, "There will be a new moon tonight; you'll be able to see the path clearly on your way home."

Makosana was tiring, and her movements became

slower and slower; she opened her mouth, gasping for air. Her chanting became almost inaudible, and her body sagged to the ground.

"Clap harder!" ordered the *inyanga* fiercely.

But it was too late. Makosana fell to the ground and lay dripping with perspiration.

"Stand back!" shouted the *inyanga* as everyone bent over her. "She'll be all right soon. It's a good omen for her. She has now finished her two years of study with me and can go back to her kraal."

She turned to Nomusa. "On your way home, please stop at Makosana's kraal on the second hill from here. Inform her father, he of the Zungu clan, to prepare a feast for his daughter's homecoming, in three sleeps. Tell him it is a message from her teacher."

As Nomusa and Themba got up to go, they saw the *inyanga* smear Makosana's forehead, cheeks, arms and chest with a mixture of the goat's blood and some medicine.

Makosana sat up bewildered, not sure where she was.

The witch doctor darted into her hut, soon returning with something in her hand. She called to Nomusa and Themba, already going out the kraal. "Wait, here's something to protect you on the way home."

She handed them two bead necklaces, one blue and white, the other red and white. Attached to each was the claw of an animal. "The red one with the lion's claw is for Themba. It will bring you good luck. Tell your father, Chief Zitu, that I thank him for the goat. Greet-

ings to your *Ugogo* and mothers. Stay well."

Nomusa and Themba were thrilled with their gifts. They helped fasten the necklaces on each other's neck, bowed gratefully to the *inyanga,* and waved good-by to the students.

They left the kraal, confident that nothing bad could happen to them now.

Chapter 8

*H*AU! Nomusa, we're lucky!'' exclaimed Themba. He fingered the beads happily.

"Now we don't have to be afraid of *any-thing* at all!"

"Don't depend on it too much, little brother. We must be as careful and watchful as ever, though our neck-laces may be helpful. It's not often one can have a leopard or lion claw to hang on a necklace," answered Nomusa.

They walked quickly. Turning her glance to the sky from time to time, Nomusa worried about the darkness that would descend upon them.

"It's getting late," she said. "I hope we won't have trouble finding Makosana's kraal."

"There will be a new moon," Themba reminded her. "By the way, Nomusa, we mustn't forget the marker for the honey bird."

"We won't be going that way now. Our path lies in that direction," she told him, pointing to a hill beyond.

"I see smoke!" exclaimed Themba, staring in the distance.

Nomusa shaded her eyes with her hand and looked hard. "I wonder where it's coming from? Let's take this short cut to Makosana's kraal."

They left the narrow trail and cut across a wide bare field, their eyes fixed on the thin ribbon of smoke. Themba ran ahead and stumbled.

"Don't depend too much on that lion's claw!" warned Nomusa.

Sheepishly, Themba waited for her. Passing a shrub

with blue flowers, Nomusa plucked one. As she did so, a soapy sap bubbled from its stem. She rubbed it on the palm of her hand and exclaimed, "Let's take back a piece of this plant to *Umama*. The sap is as good as soap for washing one's hair."

While she was breaking off a branch, Themba ran to a rocky mound so he could look down into the valley. "Hurry," he called, "I see some people working around a fire next to the stream."

Nomusa hurried over to join him, when something the color of red earth slid out from under a large stone. Frightened, she jumped back, shouting, "Look out, Themba! There's a cobra!"

The cobra, almost two feet long, threaded its way to another pile of stones nearby, its body rippling like a stream of water.

"*Awu!*" exclaimed Themba, relieved when it vanished. "The *inyanga's* necklaces did protect us, see!"

Nomusa nodded, saying, "I believe I shall become an *inyanga*. Then I can be useful to people in sickness and trouble, and to animals, too. I hope I begin having lots of dreams soon and feel the itching in my shoulders."

Now Themba noticed the lengthening evening shadows and he said, "It's getting dark."

Despite the charmed necklaces, they watched the path more carefully than ever, skirting any pile of stones. They were soon in the valley below and saw three men crouched around a hot fire in a hollow. It was this that had sent up the clouds of smoke.

"Why, it's a smithy!" Nomusa told Themba. "They're making spears and knives and hoes and piercing irons."

The blacksmith finished pounding a piece of glowing metal with a heavy round stone, then dipped it into the stream. It made a hissing sound as it struck the cold water and sent up a plume of white steam.

Two young men were working the bellows. Its nozzle was stuck deep into the burning charcoal blowing air in. The blacksmith was just finishing a spear point.

When he saw Nomusa and Themba he greeted them. *"Sakubona!"*

"I see you, too," they answered. Nomusa said, "I have a message for the father of Makosana. Can you tell me where to find him, please?"

"You have found him already," said the blacksmith. "I am Zingu."

"I have a message for you from the *inyanga*. She says your daughter, Makosana, will return to you in three sleeps, and you can prepare the feast for her homecoming."

"Hle! You bring me good news. I have not seen my daughter for many harvests," said Zingu. "How is she?"

"She is in close communication with the *idlozi,* and

the *inyanga* says she has learned much from her teaching," said Nomusa.

"I am happy to know this," said Zingu. "I hope your father will permit you and your brother and sisters to come to the feast to celebrate her return and give thanks to our ancestors."

Then he noticed Themba's eager glance resting on a hurling spear he was making; he offered him a piece of ironstone lying on the ground.

"Thank you, *inkosi*," said Themba. "I would like to be a blacksmith like you and make spears and knives."

"That is impossible, my child. Since you do not belong to the clan of blacksmiths, you can never be one. Only my sons can learn my trade and its secrets."

Nomusa tugged at Themba to leave. "We're going, *inkosi*," she told the blacksmith. "Perhaps we shall return for the feast in honor of your daughter."

"Tell Chief Zitu that the piercing iron for the ceremony will be ready in seven sleeps," said Zingu.

A short distance from the smithy Nomusa told Themba excitedly, "The ear-piercing iron must be for Mdingi and the other boys in our district."

"Good! Then we'll have a party too. What great goings-on there are these days!" said Themba jubilantly.

"It's because of the new moon," explained Nomusa. "Won't it be wonderful to see our other grandmothers? They will surely come to the ear-piercing ceremony."

"Hurrah, then we'll see the six mothers of our six mothers!" said Themba. "It's a very important occasion, isn't it?"

"Oh, yes, very! Mdingi is becoming a man so he has to be told many things he didn't know before, and he will find out what is expected of him, from now on."

A small shadow suddenly shot past Nomusa's legs. She raised her knobkerry and hurled it with all her might.

She and Themba ran to see what it had hit, cautiously holding back to make sure there was no danger. Now they came a little closer.

"Why, it's only a rock rabbit," said Nomusa. "What a good supper he will make!"

"You got the dassie with a single blow!" said Themba proudly.

Nomusa picked up the knobkerry, then raised the rock rabbit by its long ears.

When they saw that the sun had completely dropped behind the horizon, they grew a little fearful. This was the dangerous time, when wild animals came out to prowl, looking for food and drink.

Already they could see a hyena slinking about, searching for prey. As they hurried, they often stumbled over stones and twigs lying on the indistinct path.

"I hope we don't lose our way," said Nomusa.

Now they began to hear night sounds; howls, roars, grunts. Only the birds were silent. Nomusa and Themba began to run, hand in hand. Soon Nomusa felt Themba slowing down; he was tired and panting, but Nomusa would not stop.

"Little brother, we're almost home," she told him. "Please don't slow down. I can see our kraal."

"Oh-I-can't-go-any-further. I'm-out-of-breath," he gasped.

"Please, please, don't stop. We're in danger out here alone," urged Nomusa.

Now she saw his legs buckling. She grabbed him and hoisted him onto her back along with the dassie. Her steps became unsteady with the load on her back, and she wondered if she could go on. Faltering, she was on the point of stopping, when she saw someone running toward them.

Nomusa felt her throat tighten. At least it wasn't a wild beast, she comforted herself.

It was Mdingi! Overjoyed to find her, he cried, *"Awu,* Nomusa! How worried we have been about you and Themba! Are you all right?" and he took Themba from her.

"Oh, Mdingi, how happy I am to see you," she said. "And I'm glad you have your spear with you. How did you happen to come?"

"When we came home with the cattle and you were not yet back, *Ubaba* told me to go out and look for you. *Yo,* I see a rabbit on your back. You have not forgotten how to be a hunter."

In their kraal they were welcomed lovingly by their father, mothers, sisters and brothers. And there, too, was *Ugogo,* smiling happily because of their safe return. She put her arms around Nomusa and Themba and said, "This time *you* will undoubtedly have many stories to tell me!"

Chapter 9

*I*T WAS BARELY daylight three days later
when Nomusa, with Dube perched on her
shoulder, bent over the sleeping Themba
and shook him gently.

"What do you want?" he mumbled drowsily.

"Come, Themba, I'll tell you outside," she whispered.

Reluctantly he slid out from under his kaross and quietly followed Nomusa out of the hut.

Outdoors she told him, *"Ubaba* said that because we came home safely, and I was able to get the rabbit with the knobkerry, we can go to Makosana's celebration. As soon as we get *Umama's* water and firewood, we can leave."

They strode along to the stream, taking turns holding Dube, who munched a carrot noisily. Today they were quick and returned promptly. They found their mother making the mealie porridge. She told them, "Eat well now, before you go. I don't want you to shame us by appearing hungry when you are offered food. Come here, I'll rub fresh butter on you both, so you'll be clean and beautiful."

Bala tugged at her mother's skirt. "Smear butter on me, too, *Umama."*

Nomusa wiped off some of the butter from her own body and smeared it on Bala's fat belly. She said, "Now you look beautiful, too, and you smell better, little sister."

"Take me to the party," coaxed Bala.

"You are still too little," explained Nomusa. "When

you are as big and strong as Themba, you'll be able to walk longer distances."

Nomusa caught sight of Sisiwe as they were leaving the kraal yard. She called to her, *"Hi,* my sister, would you like to go with Themba and me to Makosana's party? She has just become an *inyanga."*

"If my mother can spare me, I'll gladly come," Sisiwe said.

She ran back to her hut and soon returned, looking happy. Nomusa knew she could go. But now Themba's face fell. The two girls would gossip and giggle on the way, forgetting about him. He'd seen that happen before.

Themba ran up to Nomusa to get her attention and said, "Wait, I forgot my bow and arrows to protect the two of you."

Themba felt more and more ignored and forgotten, as Nomusa and Sisiwe chatted along the way about the approaching wedding and all the preparations for it.

Sisiwe was telling Nomusa how much trouble Khotiza had caused Sigazi until he had won her.

"She was right," declared Nomusa. "It's not proper

to show a suitor quickly that you care for him. *Umama* says he will value you less. He must suffer a little because of you."

At this Themba exploded, "Then I'll *never* marry. Girls are mean!"

Nomusa and Sisiwe burst out laughing.

"If you don't marry, Themba, you won't have any children," said Nomusa. "Then who will remember you when you are no longer alive? You won't even be an ancestral spirit."

Sisiwe said, "Khotiza is worrying about the delay in the wedding because of the bargaining about the number of cows."

"Will there be a fight now between our clan and Sigazi's?" asked Themba eagerly.

Nomusa ignored the question and said, "For Khotiza's sake and ours, I hope it will soon be settled so we can have the wedding and see all our friends and relatives from the other kraals."

"Damasi will come to the wedding, won't he?" said Themba.

Nomusa blushed and turned her head away.

Sisiwe giggled and said, *"Yo,* my sister, I see it won't be long before you will be sending a love letter of white beads to someone."

They had now reached the smithy, but today only cold ashes filled the hollow in the ground. As they went up the slope of the hill, they heard loud voices from above. At the kraal entrance a large group of people were waiting. They called, *"Sakubona! Usaphila!"* They were treated respectfully, for they were the children of the chief.

The younger children crowded around Nomusa, Sisiwe, and Themba, examining everything about them with their eyes. They asked to hold Dube, who was passed from child to child; soon he grew nervous with their overwhelming affection, uneasy from the pressure of so many little hands.

"Where did you get the little monkey?" they asked.

Some asked about the lion and leopard claws on their necklaces and Themba told them marvelous tales of their remarkable powers.

Zingu kept looking through the kraal entrance impatiently. He turned to Nomusa and said, "The beer and the ram are ready. Are you sure the *inyanga* said my daughter is coming home today?"

"Yes, *inkosi*," assured Nomusa. "There is no mistake."

More neighbors filed in and soon the kraal yard was full of people talking and waiting. As time passed and Makosana did not appear, Nomusa herself became uneasy. She could see Zingu and the others casting questioning glances at her.

$\mathcal{S}$HE'S COMING!" shouted Themba.

Everyone looked toward the path leading up to the kraal. Escorting Makosana was the *inyanga,* with additional goat gall bladders bobbing in her hair, more bead necklaces around her neck, a wider belt of beads, ornaments decorating her arms and legs.

Makosana, dressed like an *inyanga,* was covered with white clay, her left eyelid painted red, the other black. One gall bladder was stuck in her hair, a single strip of goatskin was crisscrossed over her bosom. She, too, carried a gnu-tail wand-stick, but instead of a shield, she held a short spear in honor of her father's profession.

The crowd grew absolutely still as she approached. This was a great moment for Zingu and his wives. It was difficult for Nomusa to tell which was Makosana's own mother, for all the mothers seemed equally excited and proud; but Nomusa soon saw that the plumpest one, and the one to whom Makosana bore the greatest resemblance, was her mother.

The witch doctor and Makosana bowed solemnly as they entered. Leading Makosana to Zingu, she said, "Your daughter has learned well and has finished her training with me. She knows how to find and prepare medicines, how to use them, and how to keep in close communication with your *idlozi."*

"I give you thanks, *inkosikazi,"* said Zingu. "If my daughter is as expert as you say, I will give you two splendid cows in payment. Now we must test her."

Zingu's wives, in an uproar of excitement, disappeared in different directions. When they returned, Zingu said, "We are ready."

Makosana shook some snuff from a gourd at her waist into the palm of her hand and inhaled deeply; she sneezed violently, then commenced moving and hunching her shoulders as if she were doing an exercise.

"They must be itching," Themba told Nomusa, watching carefully.

"The ancestors are communicating with her," she said.

Suddenly Makosana began to jump, chanting strange words. She was no longer a shy girl but a self-confident *inyanga*. Her teacher looked on approvingly, her face proud and anxious at the same time, for her own honor and prestige were at stake.

Everyone joined in the singing and the drumming on dried cattle skins, thus whipping her up into more of a frenzy. Makosana began gliding to the other end of the kraal in search of the objects concealed by her mothers to test her.

When she drew near the hidden objects, the mothers

clapped harder to indicate she was close, fainter when not.

In a fever of excitement, everyone watched, fascinated.

"*Kawula!* Stop!" ordered Makosana.

The clapping ceased. Makosana entered a hut and before long reappeared triumphantly with an *ugubu*.

"That's it!" shouted the mothers.

Makosana held the musical instrument against her chest, her left hand striking the string of twisted sinew with a small stick of tamboukie grass. It made a pleasant sound which caused Dube's small pointed ears to stand up in wonder.

Themba tugged at Nomusa. "I'd like to learn to play that."

Nomusa answered, "Sh! It's only for girls."

Nevertheless, Themba watched closely to see how Makosana pressed the string. He saw that the tone varied according to how she held the instrument against her chest.

She sang charmingly, accompanying herself on the *ugubu*. Everyone remained quiet, listening to the sweetness of the music. Makosana had succeeded in her first test. When she had finished singing and playing, she handed the instrument to Nomusa to hold. Dube pulled at the string with one finger and was so startled by the twanging note that he hid under Nomusa's arm.

Makosana began to twitch and jerk again, looking around her. The witch doctor watched her proudly, less anxious than before, and clapped vigorously as she began a dance. Helped along by the loud and soft clappings, Makosana had her second test end in triumphant manner even sooner than the first. She rushed back from one of the huts with the second hidden object, a small brown and white courting shield.

Zingu and Makosana's own mother exchanged satisfied glances. But before the feast could begin, or the *inyanga* be paid, there was one more test. The wave of excitement was felt even by Dube, and he fidgeted restlessly in Nomusa's arms.

Themba, uneasy, brought his hand up to his lion claw attached to his necklace. He had gotten into the habit of touching it whenever he felt worried. The lion claw was gone!

He looked down to see if it had fallen off; swiftly he went down on his hands and knees feeling the loose earth around his feet.

Nomusa noticed him and asked, "What are you looking for?"

"*Yo,* my lion claw is gone!"

"Gone? But I saw it on your necklace a little while ago."

While the others followed Makosana with their clapping, Nomusa and Themba made a thorough search where he had been standing. There were tears in his eyes as the search became fruitless.

"I've got an idea," consoled Nomusa. "Let's ask Makosana to help us find it. She is an expert now."

As if guessing her thought, Makosana came running in her direction. She pointed at Dube with her wand-stick, dancing wildly around them. She shouted, "Something precious is lost! It must be returned—right away!"

Nomusa and Themba were astonished. The people in the kraal frowned. Had someone stolen something?

"The boy's lion claw is missing!" Makosana announced.

Zingu's wives were especially dismayed by the loss. If it was one of their children who had taken something belonging to another, especially from the son of their chief, it would be a terrible disgrace.

Makosana suddenly ran off and was gone longer than usual. The clapping and drumming continued as they waited for her to return. Finally, she rushed back with a beautifully made hoe held high in the air for all to see. She had completed her third test.

There was a ripple of approval: "É! É! É!"

Themba was disappointed. He had thought that Makosana would return with his precious lion's claw, and it was only a hoe her father had made. Now that she had completed her three tests, she certainly would not bother about his loss.

Everyone came up to Makosana, congratulating her; her teacher's face showed her deep pride in her pupil's achievements.

Zingu came to the *inyanga* with two cows and said, "Here are two of my best cows. Now we shall feast on a fat ram. First, however, we must serve our *idlozi* some meat and beer. The grown people will please go to the hut of Makosana's mother, the children go to the hut of my Great Wife."

Woefully Themba said to Nomusa, "Makosana said nothing more about my lion claw."

"Perhaps she's thinking about it," said Nomusa reassuringly.

Nomusa and Themba were entering the Great Wife's hut when Makosana called to them, "Come to my mother's hut. I have something to tell you."

They entered and were invited to sit on the women's side. Dube peeped out from under Nomusa's arm to see the strangers.

Makosana suddenly pointed her wand-stick at Dube and declared, "Your pet has something in his right paw."

Nomusa looked and saw it rolled up into a tight fist. She tried to open it, but he tugged his paw away. Makosana then offered him a piece of squash.

Immediately, he reached for it with his left paw, but she refused to give it to him until he reached for it with his right. As he did so, something fell to the floor. Themba looked down and saw his lion claw.

"Dube!" exclaimed Nomusa in amazement.

The *inyanga* came over to Nomusa and Themba. She said, "The lion claw must have dropped off because Themba touches and handles it so much. It is good that your pet found it. Here, let me tie it on again."

"*Ke!* Thank you, *inkosikazi*," said Themba, delighted.

The feasting began. Makosana's mother passed around pieces of the roasted ram with jugs of weak beer for the women and children.

Zingu, served first, took his stronger beer and poured

some of it on the earth floor for the ancestors. He also laid aside the choicest bits of meat for them.

The smoke from the blazing hearth fire rose thickly into the darkened thatch above. A fat beetle dropped from the ceiling at Nomusa's feet, and the witch doctor exclaimed, "That's a sign of good luck, Nomusa. If you dry the beetle and wear it around your neck, then if there is a drought, you can throw it into a river or stream and cause the rain to come."

"*Yo!* Chief Zitu's daughter is lucky!" exclaimed the girls enviously.

$\mathcal{N}$OMUSA was determined not to be caught far
from their kraal when the sun set, and she
left Makosana's feast in plenty of time to get
home early.

Sisiwe and Themba took turns holding Dube while
Nomusa kept the beetle cupped in her hands. She turned
to Sisiwe, saying, "Do you remember the time of the

terrible drought a few harvests ago?"

"How could I forget it? It was the time *Ubaba* sent for the rain doctor," said Sisiwe.

"Oh, tell me about it," begged Themba.

Nomusa began, "First a woman rain doctor was sent for. Loudly she commanded the clouds to send rain. A sheep was roasted and offered up to the heavens, but no rain came."

"Then what happened?" asked Themba.

"Ubaba sent some of the older boys to catch an *intsingize* bird, because it is a bird that doesn't fear thunder. When he was caught, he was killed and thrown into a pool of water in the hope that the hard heavens would soften and weep tears at his death."

"And then did it rain?" asked Themba eagerly.

"Yes, and too much! Our parched land grew swollen in the torrents of rain," said Nomusa. "And now a heaven-doctor had to be sent for, to lessen the power of the storm. He tried to sweep it away with a brush, then he sprinkled the medicines in the cattle enclosure, in front of the huts and the kraal yard, so the lightning wouldn't strike. He puffed medicine out of his mouth and shouted at the lightning to go out to sea. After a while the storm stopped."

They walked along in silence for a moment; then Themba asked, "Who is that going toward Damasi's kraal?"

His sisters shaded their eyes, trying to see. Soon they could make out that it was a young woman carrying something in her hand, instead of on her head. She was coming toward them, and they waited.

"Who can it be?" wondered Nomusa.

Sisiwe exclaimed, "*Yo,* it's Buselapi!"

"What's she doing wound up in all that cloth? She even has something covering her feet," said Themba.

"Let's go to her," suggested Sisiwe. "She has been away in a big city studying something, but I don't know what."

Nomusa was surprised that Sisiwe had never told her this before.

They walked toward each other and met on a grassy crosspath, offering polite greetings. Themba examined the stranger discreetly; he thought her clothing was very unattractive.

He blurted out, "Where is your navel cord?"

"I'm from the kraal of Vusumuzi, in Umbumbulu," she answered. "And where is your navel cord?" she asked, pinching Themba's cheek.

"Near Isipingo," he said. "My father is Chief Zitu, and he has six wives. How many has yours?"

"One," said Buselapi. "He is a Christian."

"Only one wife!" exclaimed Themba. He was sure

her father must be a very poor man.

While Sisiwe engaged Buselapi in conversation, Themba turned to Nomusa and said, "It must be very lonely in her kraal with only one mother. We are much luckier with our seven grandmothers, six mothers, and so many brothers and sisters."

"You mustn't count things, Themba," said Nomusa sharply. "It's bad luck!"

Sisiwe told Nomusa and Themba, "Buselapi is a nurse now."

"*Yo!*" they said, wondering what that meant.

Buselapi explained, "I have been learning how to help and take care of sick people."

"Like an *inyanga?*" asked Nomusa, interested.

"Better than an *inyanga,*" laughed Buselapi.

"*Hau!*" exclaimed Nomusa, amazed at her boastfulness and lack of modesty.

"Let's sit down over here," suggested Buselapi. "I'm tired from my long walk. I have been at Muntu's kraal for three sleeps, taking care of one of his wives. Her sickness was very heavy."

"Why didn't they send for an *inyanga?*"

"They did; she came and sacrificed a goat, smeared the sick woman with its blood and made her drink bitter medicines. But instead of getting better she grew worse."

"Worse!" exclaimed Nomusa, incredulous.

"When I arrived she was already so sick, she didn't even recognize her own children. She burned with a fever and could not speak," Buselapi told them.

"And could you do more than the *inyanga?*" asked Themba.

"Yes, I could. Someone had told Muntu about me, that I had come from the big City of Sugar, Durban, and that I had even more magical medicines and cures than an *inyanga*. Although he really didn't believe it, he was so desperate that he was willing to try me. I arrived just in time."

"What did you do?" inquired Nomusa.

"As soon as I arrived, I opened my bag and took out my glass stick to put in her mouth, so I could find out how hot her fever was making her.

"Then I listened to the sounds in her chest with this instrument, and I could hear her heartbeats growing fainter and fainter. It was serious, and I feared I was too late. Right away I began using my most powerful medicines to drive out the germs that were making her sickness so heavy."

"You mean the evil spirits? Is that what the white man calls germs?" inquired Sisiwe.

"And did you dance and chant to drive away the evil-spirit germs and communicate with the *idlozi?*" asked Themba. "How your shoulders must have itched!"

Buselapi chuckled, and said, "There was a time when I, too, believed that sickness came as a punishment or curse; I, too, watched the *inyanga* mix her mysterious medicines, dance, chant, and sacrifice animals. Sometimes she was successful; if not, she said the curse was too great, and she was powerless against it."

Nomusa interrupted. "*Inyangas* are very clever people; they can find lost things and even guess a person's thoughts."

"Quite true," agreed Buselapi, "and I can tell what you are thinking, too," and she put her arm around Nomusa's shoulders, smiling kindly at her. "You're thinking you would like to become an *inyanga* and that I ought not to say such disrespectful things about them.

Isn't that so?'' Buselapi inquired, amused.

Nomusa nodded shyly and admitted, ''I don't understand what kind of magic medicines you got in Durban that are better than an *inyanga's*. What makes them so powerful?''

''One of the magic medicines I learned about from the white man is called penicillin.'' Buselapi waited to see the effect of the strange word on her audience.

''Pen-i-cil-lin?'' they repeated, pronouncing the word with difficulty.

''Is this a medicine found on a bush in the veld? Tell me what it looks like, and I'll use it when I'm an *inyanga,*'' said Nomusa.

''No, it doesn't come from a bush, nor from flowers or roots. It comes from a mold,'' said Buselapi seriously.

''You mean a mold like that which covers mealies when they get too old and are turning bad?'' asked Nomusa.

''Exactly!'' answered Buselapi, impressed by Nomusa's intelligence.

''Well, then, I can take the mold from the old mealies and use it for medicine. That is good to know,'' said Nomusa, greatly pleased. She turned to Sisiwe and said, "My sister, when we get home let's begin scraping it off the spoiled mealies and save it!"

"But mealie mold isn't the right kind, Nomusa. Penicillin has to be made from a special mold, and then it looks like this," said Buselapi.

Out of her bag she took a small bottle. It contained a colorless liquid that looked like water to Nomusa, Sisiwe, and Themba.

Nomusa examined it carefully through the glass. "And does the sick person swallow this magical medicine?" she asked.

"No," replied Buselapi. "It's not swallowed."

"Do you rub it on the sick person?" asked Sisiwe.

"No, it's neither rubbed on nor swallowed."

"But if it's neither rubbed on nor swallowed, how can the pen-i — " and Themba stumbled over the word, "help someone who is sick?"

It was like a guessing game, all of them trying to find the right answer.

"I'll tell you," said Buselapi patiently. "When there is heavy sickness, I pour some of the penicillin liquid into

this glass tube which has a needle on the end of it. The point of the needle has a small hole in it, like the fangs of a black mamba. See?"

Nomusa, Sisiwe and Themba bent over the glass tube and needle to examine it closely.

Buselapi continued, "You know that when a snake bites a person his fangs make a hole in the skin and the poison oozes out of the fangs into it, often causing a person to die. So, when I put the penicillin into a sick person with this needle, the penicillin acts as a poison for the germs that are causing the sickness. The magic medicine kills the germs, and the sick person gets well."

As if repeating a lesson, Nomusa said, "The snake's poison kills the person, but the penicillin kills the germs and not the person. *Yo!*" She was greatly impressed.

"Really!" exclaimed Themba.

Nomusa turned earnestly to Buselapi and said, "If you will tell me the magic medicines you have learned from the white man, I'll become the cleverest of all the *inyangas* in Zululand!"

"I would gladly tell you, Nomusa, but first you would have to go to school, as I did. You would have to learn to read and write; then you could find out things in books, understand what your teachers tell you. You could help others with what you learned. It would be a fine thing if you became a nurse instead of an *inyanga,*" said Buselapi.

"Became a nurse?" repeated Nomusa, amazed.

"Yes, then you would know about germs and how they cause different sicknesses; you would learn the best way to set a broken arm or leg so it wouldn't grow crooked; you would find out what to do about a bad cut so it would heal without poisoning the blood. And many more things, but now I am tired and must go."

They all rose, brushing bits of the earth from their bodies. Buselapi touched Dube's paw gently, saying,

"See, Nomusa, your little pet has a bad sore."

"Give him the fang of penicillin," commanded Themba. "Let's poison his germs!"

"His paw doesn't need penicillin, but I have something else that will be good for it, though it does smell terrible."

From a covered jar she took out a yellow salve and spread it gently on Dube's sore paw.

Nomusa said gratefully, "Thank you, Buselapi, and go well."

"Remain well, all of you," she answered and put her capable hand on Nomusa's arm. "I hope, Nomusa, you will become a nurse instead of an *inyanga*. Our people need you, more than you know."

They touched fingers and parted, going in opposite directions. Nomusa grew so quiet and thoughtful on the way home that Themba decided Sisiwe was better company. As in a dream, Nomusa followed behind them. She was thinking about everything Buselapi had told them, especially about wanting her to go to school and become a nurse.

It was something she had never thought of before.

Chapter 12

*N*OMUSA was busy grinding mealies outside the hut; her velvety skin glistened with perspiration, for the sun was hot.

Kneeling in front of the grinding stone, she threw her weight back and forth on the stone roller, crushing the dried kernels that would become beer, porridge, corncakes, and other delicious things.

Close by, Bala was playing with Dube. They raced for the mealie kernels which sometimes bounced off the grinding stone. Dube was enjoying the game and kept stuffing the kernels into his mouth until his cheeks were as puffed out as if he had mumps.

Everyone in the kraal was especially busy this morning, and there was much bustling in and out of the huts. Nomusa stopped grinding to rest for a moment and saw Sisiwe in front of her hut shelling beans.

Nomusa called out to her, "The day after tomorrow, the moon will be full, my sister."

"Yes, I know," Sisiwe answered. "Yesterday was *Ubaba's* day to visit our mother, and he told her that the headman has been sent to invite our neighbors to bring their boys of the right age for the ear-piercing at the same time as Mdingi." She walked over to Nomusa and squatted beside her.

Themba came running. "My sisters, I can see people with small animals coming across the hills to our kraal. They are carrying beer jugs and baskets of things."

"They are bringing them for the *qhumbuza*," said Nomusa.

Not long afterwards, the neighbors Themba had seen in the distance began entering the kraal. Chief Zitu smiled, welcoming them.

Nomusa stood up to see better, her shining eyes searching through the throng of visitors. Ah, there he was! Nomusa had caught sight of Damasi walking behind his father. He, too, seemed to be looking for someone. Then he saw Nomusa, and his face brightened.

Nomusa blushed, trembling a little; she lowered her head, covering her face with her hands to conceal her confusion.

"See, Nomusa, Damasi is here," Themba told her. "He has his earplugs already, but he doesn't look like a man yet!"

"*Tula!*" cautioned Nomusa. "He may hear you."

Zitu led the guests to his own hut, calling his wives to bring extra sitting mats and strong beer.

When Nomusa's mother stuck her head through her hut entrance, Nomusa said, "We have guests, *Umama*. We must bring mats and beer to *Ubaba's* hut."

Sisiwe ran to her hut to tell her mother, in case she hadn't heard.

Within the hut, the men chatted and laughed, drank beer and smoked, the older boys listening and drinking weaker beer. On the other side of the hearth, Sisiwe nudged Nomusa, saying, "Damasi is here."

Nomusa tried to look indifferent.

"He is looking at you," whispered Sisiwe, "and he is wearing huge earplugs."

The evening before the *qhumbuza* ceremony, the ear-piercing doctor arrived to stay overnight. He had come in advance to make sure everything was in good order for the ceremony.

The boys whose ears were to be pierced had to spend the night in the same hut with him. This was to prevent them from coming into contact with anyone or anything that might make them unclean; otherwise their ears might fester and get sore after the piercing.

That same night, Zitu slept in his own hut. He had to be by himself and think about important matters. In the morning he would make suitable offerings to the ancestors.

Nomusa watched *Ugogo* bustling about, sometimes

in her own hut, sometimes in the one where Mdingi and the other boys were. Nomusa wondered what kind of wise advice *Ugogo* was giving them. She wished she were a boy so she could find out what they were told when they were about to become men.

Like a sentinel, *Ugogo* now stood at the kraal entrance scanning the hills, looking for something. Nomusa came over and put her arm around her grand-

mother's waist, asking, "What are you looking for, dear *Ugogo?*"

Straining to see, she did not answer at first; then she pointed, *"Hau!* They come!"

Nomusa looked. *"Yo,* I see, too!"

To her great delight she saw her six other grandmothers slowly and steadily making their way from the valley below up to their kraal.

Chapter 13

At Ugogo's delighted cry, Zitu's six wives came running, followed by Nomusa's many sisters and brothers, hopping up and down in happy excitement.

Nomusa had never really counted how many sisters and brothers she had. It was considered bad luck to do so; not that they didn't know immediately if a child was

missing, but it was better not to invite trouble by count-
ing your age, the number in your family, or tell how many
animals you had.

At last the six barefooted grandmothers padded up
the last bit of the path to the kraal entrance. Some were
puffing from the exertion of the climb and leaned heavily
on their long walking sticks. Others strode along like
young women.

Nomusa ran forward to help Fifth *Ugogo* with her
heavy basket of sweet potatoes which she carried on top
of her head as gracefully as a girl. Next to *Ugogo,* her
father's mother, Nomusa loved her best of all the grandmothers.

"I see Nomusa, daughter of my daughter," greeted
Fifth *Ugogo* warmly, and put her free arm around her.

Nomusa said, *"Sakubona,"* and stretched out her
hands to take the basket from her.

The older children ran forward to meet their grandmothers and relieve them of their overflowing baskets,
calabashes and clay pots.

"Welcome, welcome," called *Ugogo* to the visiting
grandmothers. As each one entered the kraal, dressed in

softened oxskins fastened under their arms, *Ugogo* placed her hand affectionately on their shoulders. Pointing to her hut, she invited them to go in.

The children deposited their grandmothers' gifts in front of *Ugogo's* hut and waited outside. When the seven grandmothers went in, together with their six married daughters and the older grandchildren, the younger ones were told to stay outdoors.

Themba looked forlorn at being left outside, especially when Dube struggled to follow Nomusa.

Nomusa and her sisters spread out additional mats. The hearth fire was bright; the cook pot boiled briskly and the hut was filled with the good smell of food.

When everyone was seated, there was no sound save that of the scuffling and stamping of a baby calf in the pen.

It was not good manners to ply one's guests with conversation and questions as soon as they arrived. They should be given a chance to catch their breath, rest, size up people — in a discreet way, of course. Everyone knew this and bided his time.

After a suitable interval, *Ugogo* drew a long breath, coughed lightly, and unfolded her hands. She turned to the other grandmothers with a soft chuckle, and asked, "Did all go well with you along the way? Was your journey not too tiring?"

Eyes that had been respectfully lowered were now raised. The proper interval had been observed; the silence was broken. The hut now resounded with the hum of conversation and laughter while the grandmothers inspected grandchildren, and the grandchildren inspected their grandmothers.

Nomusa found a place between her mother and Fifth *Ugogo*. She saw Fifth *Ugogo* looking at Makanya with great pride and pleasure in her soft brown eyes. They talked quietly together for a time, then Fifth *Ugogo* asked Nomusa's mother, "Are you beautiful, my daughter?"

"Yes, *Umama,*" she answered softly. "I expect the new baby in three moons."

"*Yo,* I am happy to hear it!" exclaimed Fifth *Ugogo,* beaming at the good news. "It was time."

The grandmothers gossiped with each other about weddings, bride-dowries, quarrels, sickness, charms, magic, and bargains in the market.

To all this the children listened attentively; it was from listening to such conversations that they learned what went on in the Zulu world, and discovered what was expected of people.

After a suitable interval, the mothers returned to their huts; they soon came back with food they had been preparing for the visitors. They brought *amasi,* the clotted milk, crushed mealies boiled with *amasi,* green herbs mixed with crushed mealies, cornbeer dregs in boiled mealies, small black beans, a kind of spinach, and wild figs.

Themba came running in after his mother with a basket of large roasted caterpillars and broiled flying ants, the greatest delicacies of all.

The hut was dark, illuminated only by the hearth fire and the tiny light coming from a stone dish filled with melted fat, which hung on the center post. The smoke from the wick of dried grass drifted lazily up into the thatch.

The children, leaning against their grandmothers, were soothed by their melodious voices and tender embraces. It made no difference to them which was the mother of their own mother. All the grandmothers were very dear to the children.

The brothers who had returned from herding and milking the cows now entered the hut to greet their grandmothers. *Ugogo* told them, "Eat, my children. It is good, and there is more than enough."

She turned to resume her conversation with the other grandmothers. "I have told the boys whose ears are to be pierced that if they didn't have it done, they would remain foolish children, and good for nothing."

"Did you tell them to work hard, to obey their elders and love their cattle?" asked Third *Ugogo*.

"That I have, and I have also told them to help their fathers."

"And did you remind them," asked Fourth *Ugogo,* "not to sit too much by the fire lest it burn their legs and cause them to catch cold from hugging the warmth more than they should?"

"That I have, also. And I told them that from now on they must always sit with their knees drawn up, not flat like women, ready to rise in a moment."

Some of the smaller children began to nod sleepily,

for it was getting late and the hut had become too warm. The air was thick with a mixture of odors coming from their bodies greased with fat and red ochre, from food cooking, and from the animal pen. Some of the children stretched out and fell sound asleep. When their mothers tried to take them back to their huts, they protested, saying, "Our *ugogos* haven't told us a story yet."

Fifth *Ugogo,* smoothing her hide skirt, said, "I'll tell one."

Everyone in the hut grew quiet, their eyes fixed on

her expressive face. She began, "Once upon a time, the birds decided to choose a king. So they called a meeting of the council and said, 'The bird that can fly the highest shall be king,' and a day was set for the contest. Just before the contest began, the *ucilo,* which is the tiniest of all the birds and lives on small grasshoppers, secretly crept under the wing of an eagle.

"Now the race was on, and the eagle flew higher and higher, soaring above all the others. Just as he was thinking that he had outdistanced the other birds, and that he would now be king, out flew the little *ucilo,* outdistancing the eagle.

"But the other birds, as well as the eagle, had seen what a trick the *ucilo* had played on them, and they were angry. They decided to punish him for being unfair, but before they could do so he escaped into a hole.

"Choosing an owl, they told him to guard the hole so that the *ucilo* would not escape again. But after a while the owl grew sleepy and he thought to himself, 'There's no harm in closing one eye while I keep watch with the other.' So, he kept watch, first with one eye then with the other, until finally, when he shut his right eye, he forgot to open his left. This was just the chance the *ucilo* was waiting for, and when he saw the owl had closed both eyes and was fast asleep, he ran out of his hole and got away. Well, when the other birds found out what had happened, they were very, very displeased with the owl for letting the *ucilo* escape.

"From that time, the owl has been in such disgrace that he only comes out at night." She unfolded her hands and said, "I have finished."

The children began to stir, some rubbing their eyes

and yawning. It was time to go back to their huts. Sleep-ily they smiled their thanks to Fifth *Ugogo.*

They followed their mothers out of the warm hut into the bracing night air, the deep blue sky sprinkled with many stars.

An owl hooted in the distance. Tonight it sounded especially unhappy and forlorn, thought the children, because of Fifth *Ugogo's* story.

Scratching his head sleepily, Themba yawned loudly and mumbled, "That was a good story Fifth *Ugogo* told us."

"*Tula!* Bala is already asleep. We'll talk about it in the morning," Nomusa said.

"*Ke,* very well. Good night, *Umama,*" he called softly, and curled up on his mat, pulling the goatskin cover up to the tip of his nose.

Nomusa lay down on her mat, too, pulled the kaross over herself, and put Dube on top of it.

Except for the swish and rustle in the thatch of the hut, all was quiet. Nomusa found it soothing to hear the field mice chasing each other in their nightly play across the roof.

$\mathcal{N}$OMUSA WAS not quite awake when she felt a tickle on her ear; then she heard an indistinct voice murmuring something close to her head. At first she thought it was Dube and she waved her hand in the air to brush him away. But now she clearly heard, "Get up, Nomusa. This is the day of the *qhumbuza;* let's go outdoors and see what's going on."

Themba was bending over her eagerly. Dube turned his head from one to the other, hoping Themba would succeed in getting her up.

She rose, rolled up her mat, folded the kaross, and put them away neatly. She saw that her mother, Bala and Kangata were still asleep, so she beckoned to Themba and Dube. They left the hut quietly.

Nomusa sniffed the fresh, fragrant air, then looked across the green hills glistening with the abundant morning dew. She saw acacia trees waving their graceful yellow blossoms; spider webs covered with tiny dew drops, attached to the euphorbia and thorn fence of the kraal, twinkled like diamonds in the strong sunlight.

She caught sight of *Ugogo* coming out of the boys' hut. *Ugogo* beckoned to her and Themba, and they ran to see what she wanted.

"When you go to the stream this morning, please take a larger jar. I need more water than usual."

"And I will bring you more firewood, *Ugogo,*" said Themba, eager to help.

On the way to the stream Nomusa met Khotiza, a hoe on her shoulder.

"I see you are on your way to your garden, Khotiza," said Nomusa. "I am glad to have your company because soon you will be a married woman and leave us. Are you almost ready with the songs and dances you are composing for your wedding?"

"Oh, yes, Nomusa. I shall have to begin practicing them with the girls in my bridal party. Would you like to hear one of the songs, and see one of the dances?"

Khotiza laid her hoe on the ground and commenced clapping her hands to start up the rhythm. She began to sway her body gracefully, then sang:

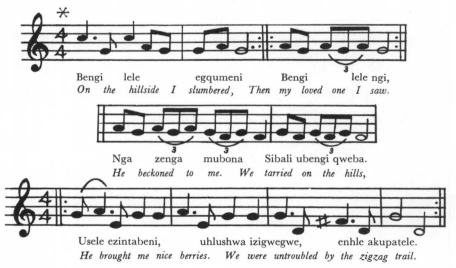

Bengi lele egqumeni Bengi lele ngi,
On the hillside I slumbered, Then my loved one I saw.

Nga zenga mubona Sibali ubengi qweba.
He beckoned to me. We tarried on the hills,

Usele ezintabeni, uhlushwa izigwegwe, enhle akupatele.
He brought me nice berries. We were untroubled by the zigzag trail.

*Music collected by R.P.M. in Zululand.
Unpublished.*

She twisted her body, stamped the ground vigorously and the dance became livelier. Then her song grew more solemn, expressing her sadness at having to leave the kraal of her father for a strange one. Her voice became excited, high-pitched, with a chorus of *"li-li-li-li-!"* over and over again.

The music was irresistible; Nomusa put down her water jar and followed Khotiza's intricate dance steps, imitating her song. She swayed, stooped, stamped, following Khotiza's movements carefully.

Panting from the exertion, Khotiza stopped and asked, "What do you think of it?"

"Yo, the song and the dance are very beautiful!" Nomusa answered, impressed by Khotiza's ability to compose them. "I hope I can do as well when I am old enough to be married."

Nomusa hoisted the water jar on the grass ring which cushioned her head and walked along humming the song she had just learned.

She stopped humming, right in the middle of a phrase and stood still when she passed the last wild fig tree. She became aware of something moving under it and she stood rooted to one spot, uneasy.

With a sigh of relief she soon relaxed and smiled when she saw what it was. Baboons! A mother baboon was walking on all fours with her baby on her back, like a tiny horseman. Nomusa saw that the mother was hunting for insects; she watched her turning over stones and quickly catching the insects hiding underneath. Once she captured a deadly scorpion and swiftly pulled off its sting before putting it into her mouth.

The baby baboon complained with grunts and peevish barks, begging for his share. Nomusa knew that baboons feared to let their young run freely on the ground because of their foolish curiosity. Rock pythons lay waiting to squeeze the life out of careless little baboons.

As she brought *Ugogo's* share of water to her, No-

musa saw her seven grandmothers standing in front of the hut, talking and laughing. Hanging on to the separate fingers of their hands were their little grandchildren, nudging each other out of the way for a better position.

"Here they come!" announced Themba, dashing to the kraal gate. Damasi entered with his father, his older brothers, and the men from neighboring kraals.

Zitu came forward to welcome and greet them. The boys who were secluded in the hut were now summoned by the ear-piercing doctor. Zitu was going to make the thanksgiving offering to their ancestral spirits.

First a male animal, an ox, was to be sacrificed. No women or girls, excepting the grandmothers who were past child-bearing age, were permitted to be near the entrance of the cattlefold, the scene of the sacrifice.

Nomusa, overwhelmed by curiosity, resented having to stay away from the ceremony. Before the moon rose, she decided to hide behind a bush higher up the hill; from here she could get a good view of the cattlefold and the ceremony. She told herself firmly, "I'm not really doing anything wrong because I'm not near enough to the *qhumbuza* to make it unclean."

The moon was rising slowly, and in a little while the ceremony would begin. Concealed, Nomusa saw the boys lined up in a row according to their age and rank. Mdingi, the son of a chief, was at the head of the line.

The ear-piercing doctor, getting ready, wiped off his sharp-pointed knife with a wad of grass. Three men grabbed Mdingi and held him firmly so he wouldn't struggle or move while the point of the knife was plunged

through the lobes of his ears, making the horizontal slit which distinguished Zulu boys and men from other tribes.

Into the slits he inserted the top of a cornstalk that had been cut into small pieces. This accomplished, he went to the next boy, wiping off his knife each time with the same grass wad.

The grandmothers uttered high-pitched delighted cries of *"li-li-li,"* to show their pride in the new full members of the family.

A boy from another kraal was now held by the three men. As the ear-piercing doctor plunged the knife point into an ear lobe, he pulled back in fright and trembled.

Nomusa was sorry for him; his lack of courage would bring disgrace to his family. How thankful she was that Mdingi had not flinched! She had always been proud of him for being able to make up delightful songs and poems; now she was proud because he was brave.

Damasi's brother, Maboko, was next. Because of the previous boy's behavior, he was grasped more firmly than the others had been. Nomusa saw Damasi's face, serious and anxious.

In her affection for Damasi, she found herself nervous about his brother.

Maboko neither moved nor winced. His eyes downcast, Damasi's brother did not show the slightest sign of pain, but stood straight and immovable.

The grandmothers continued trilling their happy songs, clapping and swaying in a dignified fashion, befitting their age.

Now that the ears of the boys had been slit, Zitu came forward and stood before them solemnly. Nomusa heard him saying, "Something very important has taken place in your lives. Your ears have been opened so you may hear and understand things better. From now on you are considered more responsible than your younger brothers, and you will be held accountable for their behavior as well as your own.

"You must love your cattle. Obey those who are older and do not trifle with women. You know now what is expected of you; you have been given good and wise advice in the hut. We hope you will never displease or anger your ancestral spirits by unworthy behavior. I have finished."

"We hear you!" cried the boys earnestly.

During the praise songs in honor of Chief Zitu, No-musa stole away. She had been greatly impressed and inspired by what she had seen. Above all, her curiosity was satisfied.

Nomusa was glad no one was in her hut when she entered; she wanted to be alone and think. Soon Themba burst into the hut chasing Dube, who had run away with his ball.

"Oh, you're here, Nomusa. Where have you been?" he asked. "Come, the *qhumbuza* is over and the feast will begin. You ought to see all the good things there are to eat! By the way, Damasi is looking for you, my sister."

When Themba left, Nomusa smiled happily to herself, hugging Dube more than usual. This time, her pet found her affection excessive, and he squirmed uncomfortably. She put him down and filled a half calabash with water. This was her mirror.

She set it down before her and looked into it. With a wooden comb she combed her short curly hair, then added another bead necklace to the ones she already wore.

She transferred the contents of her old deerskin

neckpocket to her best oxhide one, then inspected herself again in the water mirror.

When she had finished smoothing and straightening her bead apron, her bracelets, armlets and anklets, she was satisfied with her appearance and picked up Dube.

As soon as she was outdoors, Sisiwe ran to her.

"Hurry, Nomusa," she urged, "the dancing contest between the boys and girls is going to take place before the feast. Now the boys with the pierced ears can dance and eat with us."

Nomusa saw Mdingi and Damasi coming toward her. Shyly she buried her face in Dube's soft fur.

"*Hawu,* Nomusa!" greeted Mdingi gaily. "I'm a man now. Hereafter you must always obey me. See my earplugs?"

"I see them, my brother," she answered respectfully. Then she raised her twinkling eyes and laughingly said, "I shall remember to obey you, Mdingi, only if your order is sensible!"

"That's right, Nomusa!" agreed Damasi, his face full of his admiration for her. "Come and be my partner. You and I haven't danced together for a long, long time."

Chapter 15

NOMUSA and her mother were hoeing their vegetable garden. Her mother stopped working and said, "I am greatly worried about Mdingi, my daughter."

"Why, *Umama?* What is the matter?" she asked.

"It is five days since the ear-piercing ceremony, and the slits in his ear lobes are festering badly. Ever since the *qhumbuza* he has slept in the hut of the big boys, so I haven't seen him as much as usual.

"But yesterday, when he brought me the milk from our cows, he looked very sick. Something bad is happening to his ear slits."

Nomusa stopped hoeing. Fear clutched at her heart, and she grew thoughtful, silent.

Her mother sighed. "I'm afraid someone or something was unclean when the ceremony took place. Perhaps someone did not take proper care, or someone was there who should not have been."

Nomusa threw her mother a startled glance, then began hoeing energetically to hide her guilty face. Yes, thought Nomusa, reproaching herself, someone was there who should not have been! I have done a terrible thing. Oh, why am I always so curious and eager to know about everything! If only I were content to be like other girls!

She wished she had the courage to confess to her mother; tell her the cause of Mdingi's trouble.

Was Mdingi the only one whose ears had been pierced who was having this trouble, she wondered? If so, it was a sure sign that the *idlozi* had singled him out for punishment because of what she had done.

Her thoughts were interrupted when her mother said, "This is the day for your father's visit to our hut, so pick all the vegetables that are ripe. I wish to cook for him the things he especially enjoys eating. When he comes I shall speak to him about Mdingi so he can send for an *inyanga;* she will be able to tell us the cause of the bad luck which has befallen us."

Now, thought Nomusa, the *inyanga* will smell me out and tell everyone I am the cause of it. What would Damasi think of her then? Full of guilt and remorse, she turned to her hoeing with such energy that her mother asked, "Whatever is the matter with you today, Nomusa? Why are you exhausting yourself like this? Help me put the vegetables into the baskets, and we'll return to the kraal. Come, Bala, come, Dube!"

Bala and Dube had been playing tag with each other between the rows of vegetables.

As soon as they reached their hut, Nomusa began cleaning the vegetables while her mother prepared herself for Zitu's visit.

"Fetch the tobacco and beer for your father while I

put on my new oxhide skirt and beads," Nomusa was told.

Nomusa did as her mother asked. She knew how important it was to please Zitu so he would be glad to come when it was their turn for his visit.

Bala ran into the hut announcing, "*Ubaba* is coming!"

Nomusa hurried to spread out her father's sitting mat. The earth floor had been especially well-swept and rubbed down today. She saw her mother, excited, fumbling with her necklace as she tried to fasten it around her neck.

Nomusa went over to help her.

Soon they heard someone outside coughing and clearing his throat softly. It was Zitu announcing his arrival. Quickly Makanya went to the entrance to greet her husband.

"*Sakubona!*" said Zitu cheerfully.

"*Usaphila!*" welcomed his wife modestly.

Nomusa, Themba and Bala kneeled respectfully before him. He went to sit down on the bamboo mat woven especially for him.

Zitu drew Bala and Themba toward him, holding

them close. Nomusa was happy to see her father gazing at her mother so admiringly, as Makanya passed the beer and tobacco to him.

He took out his oxhorn pipe and stuffed the tobacco into it. Nomusa lighted a splinter in the hearth fire and passed it to him. For a few moments he puffed, enjoying the aroma of the tobacco.

Silent, Makanya and her children watched and waited for him to speak.

"Excellent tobacco you grow," he said appreciatively. They were delighted to have pleased him.

Soon Mdingi and Kangata entered carrying the evening pail of milk. They bowed respectfully to their father, gave Makanya the milk, then took down their sitting mats.

Zitu noticed, when they were eating, that Mdingi seemed to have no appetite and that his ears were swollen and festering. He looked across the hut to his wife, asking her a question with his eyes. Then he said, "Something has happened that should not have. How is it with you, Mdingi?"

"I fear all is not as it should be, *Ubaba*," said Mdingi

weakly. "My ears are not healing, and I can't sleep at night. But I am not the only one. Today while herding, I met Damasi's brother, Maboko, and he told me he is having the same trouble. He said his father has sent for the *inyanga*."

Nomusa grew more miserable than ever. *Yo,* she thought, so I have brought bad luck to Damasi's brother as well as to Mdingi.

Zitu sat silent, in deep thought; then he turned to Nomusa and said, "My daughter, tell the headman to send for the *inyanga*."

"I go, *Ubaba,*" said Nomusa, hurrying to deliver the message. She was glad to be outside, alone. The evening was still young when she walked across the kraal yard to her father's hut.

Suddenly, outside the kraal fence, she heard someone calling insistently. It was the voice of a woman, a familiar one.

Apparently, the headman had heard it, too, for he came running with spear ready in case of trouble. Nomusa helped him pull back the heavy wooden bars and push the gate slightly to one side to see who was there.

It was the *inyanga*. At the unexpected sight of her, Nomusa's mouth went dry. Had the witch doctor already been in communication with the *idlozi* and found out about Mdingi's ears, even before they sent for her? This very evening, the *inyanga* would surely point her out as the cause of Mdingi's punishment.

"There is trouble here, so I have come," said the witch doctor.

Nomusa bowed and said, "It is well that you have come, *inkosikazi*." She was glad, and yet she was not glad.

The *inyanga* entered Makanya's hut with Nomusa. In the soft, dim light the witch doctor looked less severe than in the daytime. This evening her face was more like that of a worried mother.

"*Bayete!*" she greeted Zitu and walked over to Makanya's side. She explained, "I have just been to see Maboko, whose ears are ailing badly. After I finished putting my medicines on them, his brother Damasi told me about Mdingi, so here I am."

"Thank you for coming," said Zitu. "It is not well with my son."

The witch doctor looked across at Mdingi and exclaimed, *"Ye-le-le!* Come here, my boy."

Mdingi raised himself feebly and knelt before her as she examined his inflamed ear cuts. The expression on her face showed plainly that she was not pleased with what she saw.

"Bring me warm water, Nomusa. I wish to soak an *uzi* root in it," she said.

While she was getting the water, the witch doctor took from the hide bag hanging from her waist something

which she put into her mouth. She began chewing it hard.

She dropped the *uzi* root in the hot water, then blew the finely chewed substance from her mouth on to Mdingi's festering ear lobes. Mdingi, his hands tightly clasped, his eyes closed with pain, did not move.

His mother tenderly placed her hand on his arm so he would feel her comforting presence. She was frightened when she felt his skin, burning with fever, and saw the deep circles under his eyes.

Inwardly she prayed to the *idlozi* to protect her oldest son, not to punish him for something that had displeased them. Nomusa could not bear to look at the suffering faces of her mother and Mdingi. She wanted to go to her father and say, *"Ubaba,* it is I who have done this to Mdingi." She would gladly endure anything to make her brother well again.

Anxious, she watched the *inyanga* wash his ear slits with the warm water. She heard her singing, *"Uye uja ho, uye uja ho, eya he he,"* over and over in a low voice.

"If only what the *inyanga* is doing works!" Nomusa prayed.

The *inyanga* stopped chanting and told Mdingi, "Tonight you must sleep in your mother's hut."

Kangata went to get Mdingi's sleeping mat and unrolled it next to Zitu. Weak and tired, Mdingi lay down on his back to protect his ailing ears. He closed his eyes wearily, licking his parched lips. Beads of perspiration stood out on his face.

With deep concern Zitu looked down at Mdingi and wiped the moisture from his brow and cheeks. "Get him his kaross," Zitu told Kangata softly.

"It is too late for me to return to my kraal now," said the witch doctor, "so I shall have to spend the night here."

"You are more than welcome," said Zitu.

Nomusa unrolled a sleeping mat for her. At a sign from her mother, Nomusa banked the hearth fire, and everyone lay down to sleep.

$\mathcal{N}$OMUSA WAS too worried and heavy-hearted to be able to fall asleep as quickly as usual. She tossed and turned, full of self-reproach and guilt.

Consequently, when she woke up in the morning, she found she had overslept. Her mother was up before her, stirring the fire and getting the cook pot ready.

Nomusa rose quickly and looked to see if the witch doctor was still asleep, but her mat was empty, and so was Zitu's and Kangata's. *Yo,* how late it must be!

Then she saw that Mdingi had not gone to herd the cattle with Kangata, a bad sign indeed.

Nomusa whispered to her mother, "How is it with Mdingi this morning, *Umama?*"

"I think it is still very bad with him, and I am afraid. He could not rise from his mat to go with Kangata. When the *inyanga* left she told me it will take a little time for her medicines and charms to work on his ears."

Mdingi was worse, then! Nomusa's throat tightened. She looked across the hut and saw how restless and miserable he was. He breathed in short gasps and was trying to throw off the kaross because of the fever that was burning him.

"Water, *Umama,*" he called in a weak voice.

Nomusa and her mother went quickly to him.

They held him up to drink from a water gourd with a narrow stem. Nomusa felt his hot dry skin against hers. Now she could see his ear lobes, more swollen and inflamed than ever.

Even his cheeks were being infected by the evil-
spirit germs. And all because of what she had done!

Suddenly, Nomusa remembered something. Buselapi!

She recalled what the nurse had told her about the
white man's magic medicine, and that it was more powerful than anything an *inyanga* had. She decided to find
Buselapi as quickly as possible.

After helping Mdingi drink, Nomusa and her

mother gently helped him lie down on the mat. Makanya brought him some thin mealie porridge, but he refused it.

Bala and Themba were now awake, getting ready to pounce on each other playfully, as they did each morning. Nomusa called to them sharply, *"Tula!"* and pointed at Mdingi. She motioned that they should go outside and play. Picking up the water jar she went outdoors.

Themba asked her, "Didn't the *inyanga* make our brother better?"

"Mdingi's sickness is heavy," she explained. "So far the *inyanga* has been powerless."

"Awu! How angry our *idlozi* must be to punish Mdingi so! What do you suppose he did?" asked Themba.

"Perhaps it's what someone else has done that brought him this trouble," she told him.

"If th*e inyanga* comes again, let's ask her to smell out the person who put this curse on our brother. That person should be severely punished for it," he declared angrily.

"You are right, Themba," said Nomusa, sadder than ever.

Sisiwe entered the kraal with her full water jug balanced on her head. When she saw Nomusa she called out, "You're very late in fetching your water today, Nomusa."

Nomusa ran up to her. "Sisiwe, you're just the one I want to see. Leave the water at your hut and hurry back. I have something terribly important to ask you."

Sisiwe quickened her leisurely gait and soon returned to Nomusa and Themba. "What is it, Nomusa?"

"It's about Mdingi," said Nomusa.

"How is it with him?" Sisiwe asked sympathetically.

"Worse! He's sicker than ever; I must find Buselapi."

"Buselapi?" repeated Sisiwe and Themba.

"Yes, and quickly, too. Do you remember what she told us about the white man's magic medicine?"

"You mean the pen-i-cil-lin?" asked Sisiwe.

"Yes, we must find her right away. Sisiwe, can you remember where Buselapi said she lives?" begged Nomusa.

Sisiwe knitted her brow, rubbing her forehead. Nomusa and Themba watched her anxiously. All at once

Sisiwe exclaimed, "Now I remember! It was Umbum-bulu!"

"Yes, yes, that's it!" cried Nomusa, greatly relieved. "I must go there at once."

"But it's far away, Nomusa," Sisiwe told her. "Besides, you can't go without *Ubaba's* permission, you know."

"I'll go and ask him now," declared Nomusa.

Themba followed her to Zitu's hut. Standing in front of the entrance, Nomusa coughed lightly and waited. There was no answer. She coughed again, more loudly, reinforced by Themba's imitation of Zitu clearing his throat.

"Come in!"

They saw their father sitting with the headman, smoking and talking about affairs in their district.

"Welcome, my children, and how is Mdingi today?" asked Zitu.

"We come with bad news, *Ubaba,*" said Nomusa.

Zitu laid down his pipe, and his face clouded.

"He is no better, then?" he asked anxiously.

"No, *Ubaba*. His sickness is very heavy. I come for

permission to bring Buselapi here," she told him.

"Buselapi? What for?"

Themba broke in, "*Ubaba,* she has a magic medicine that she says is more powerful than anything an *inyanga* has; it will make Mdingi well again."

"What is this nonsense you children are talking?" Zitu said impatiently. "If Mdingi is no better I'll call in another *inyanga* to find out who has offended the *idlozi!*"

The headman turned to Zitu. "*Inkosi,* perhaps your children speak of Buselapi, daughter of Vuzumu, from Umbumbulu. She is the one who went to the City of Sugar to learn new ways to cure sickness."

"What could she have learned that our *inyangas* do not already know?" asked Zitu disdainfully.

"Penicillin!" exclaimed Themba, proud to have gotten the word out in one piece this time.

"Pen-i — ?" Zitu could get no further. Exasperated at first, his stern expression now turned to one of vast amusement. He said to the headman, "Already Themba and Nomusa know more than I do. Have you heard of this magical medicine that the daughter of Vuzumu is using?"

"Yes, *inkosi*. The last time I carried your message to the heads of the kraals, I met Muntu and asked him about his sick wife. I knew the *inyanga* had been to see her and that she had been powerless to help her."

"Indeed!" exclaimed Zitu, interested.

The tone of Zitu's voice gave Nomusa courage to say, "Then Muntu heard of Buselapi and her magic medicines and sent for her. She told me she came barely in time and . . ."

"And she killed the germs!" interrupted Themba.

"The germs?" Zitu was puzzled.

"Yes, *Ubaba,* that's what the white man calls the evil spirits," explained Themba.

"It was with the penicillin, the magic medicine, that she killed the germs," Nomusa told him.

"*Hau!* Is it, then, powerful for everything? Let us send for Buselapi and tell her to give this wonderful medicine to our *inyangas*. If she really wishes to help her people, this is how she can do it," declared Zitu firmly.

"Then may I go and summon her, *Ubaba?*" begged Nomusa. "She'll help not only Mdingi but Maboko, who has the same sickness."

"It's a long way to Umbumbulu, my daughter, and Buselapi may even be somewhere else with a sick person. But if you wish to go, you must not go alone," Zitu cautioned.

Themba blurted out, "Oh, she will have me, *Ubaba*. I'll take my bow and arrows to protect her."

Zitu and his headman smiled. "Is it not too far for you to walk, my son?"

"*Qa,* no, *Ubaba.* I never get tired!" declared Themba.

The headman said, "I heard that Buselapi was going to Lutuli's kraal. His wife is expecting another baby and will need her help."

"And why didn't they send for an *inyanga?*" asked Zitu angrily. "I am displeased that some of our people are turning away from the customs of their ancestors. It will bring bad luck."

The headman continued, "The last time Lutuli's wife was having a baby, she had great difficulty bearing it. Although the *inyanga* came and stayed two days, the baby died and the mother was near death herself.

"That is why he sent for Buselapi, lest he lose both his wife and child this time. Buselapi has been going from kraal to kraal, explaining to our women better ways of keeping themselves and their children healthy. She teaches them what to do not only after a child is born, but before."

"Hm! So Buselapi is taking away the work of our

inyangas," said Zitu, and Nomusa saw that he was not content. *"Ke,* very well, Nomusa, go with Themba and find this Buselapi. I wish to see and speak with her. I will then decide whether to let her try the white man's magical medicine on my son. Go well, my children, and take care."

Nomusa and Themba bowed and left. Outdoors Nomusa told Themba, "Go quickly and get wood for *Umama,* and be sure to take Bala with you. I will get the water. Then we'll tell *Umama* about Buselapi."

When Sisiwe saw Nomusa returning from the stream, she ran to her. "Themba told me! I'll gladly take care of Bala and Dube and do whatever our mother wishes while you are gone."

Nomusa entered the hut with the water jar; she saw her mother putting an extra kaross over Mdingi, who was shivering with cold.

Her mother looked more worried than ever. She took the water jar from Nomusa and whispered, "We must send for another *inyanga* right away. Mdingi's sickness is growing heavier, and I am much afraid."

"Umama, I have something to tell you," said No-

musa. At first she thought she would confess, but instead she found herself telling her again about Buselapi and her magic medicine and that she had Zitu's permission to fetch her.

"So now I'm going to find her, *Umama,*" Nomusa told her.

"If your father says so, very well, but she must come quickly with her most powerful medicines. The evil spirits have entered Mdingi's head, and he is muttering things I cannot understand. I hope Buselapi's medicine will send them away. Where will you go to find her, my daughter?" asked Makanya.

"Either at Lutuli's kraal or in Umbumbulu. While I'm gone Sisiwe will help you; Bala and Dube are with her now."

"Then go well and don't delay. It's very serious now."

Nomusa ran out of the hut with Themba, hand in hand.

Chapter 17

NOT FAR FROM Damasi's kraal Themba broke
the silence by asking, "In which direction is
Umbumbulu, my sister?"

"Over there, I think," she pointed, "but first we're
going to Lutuli's kraal. Oh, I do hope Buselapi is there,
otherwise we'll have to go to her kraal, and we might
not be able to come back with Buselapi until tomorrow."

"*Awu!* By that time our brother may be beyond the power of the white man's magic medicine," said Themba gloomily.

At the edge of the long path ahead of them they saw someone walking fast. "I wonder who it is?" said Themba.

"It looks like a man," observed Nomusa.

In the still, clear air, the sound of people talking reached the ears of the person ahead of them. He turned and shouted, "*Sakubona,* Nomusa. I see you, Themba!"

"Why, it's Damasi!" exclaimed Nomusa excitedly. "*Sakubona!* Wait for us, Damasi!"

Damasi waved and waited. They ran until they reached him.

"Are your brother's ear slits better, Damasi?" asked Nomusa.

"Alas, no, they're worse, and we are greatly worried. I am on my way now to summon another *inyanga.* How is it with Mdingi?"

"*Bi!* Bad!" said Nomusa unhappily. "Themba and I are going to fetch Buselapi, the nurse. She has a magic medicine she learned from the white man which she told us is very powerful; we hope it will make Mdingi well, and Maboko, too.''

Mingled doubt and curiosity crossed Damasi's face. He said, ''I have heard about Buselapi. They say she is clever and skillful; hasn't she studied in the City of Sugar?''

''Yes, she has been to school there and has learned things to help our people. She wants me to go to school, too. She says I will find out wonderful things from books and teachers that I never knew or dreamed of,'' said No-musa.

''I'll tell you what, Nomusa. If the *inyanga* can't help Maboko this time, I'll tell my father about Buselapi. Good-by, and stay well,'' said Damasi. ''And be sure to let me know if the magic medicine helps Mdingi.''

To make up for the time lost in talking with Damasi, Nomusa began to walk so fast that Themba could not keep up with her. He no longer felt he was either her companion or protector.

After a time Nomusa brightened. *''Yo,* I see Lutuli's kraal. Are you tired, little brother?''

''Only my ears,'' he said. ''They are weary from not

hearing you speak and that's why the way seemed longer."

"If only Buselapi is there!" said Nomusa.

Nomusa hurried ahead, followed by Themba, trotting like a puppy.

In Lutuli's kraal yard, girls were grinding mealies; they stopped what they were doing to look at the unexpected visitors. Nomusa spoke to one of the girls she recognized who took her to her father's hut. There was a new baby in the hut, so Themba had to stay outside because men and boys were not allowed to enter the hut where there was a new baby; only the father was permitted to be there.

Nomusa scraped her feet carefully on the ashes in front of the hut, a necessary precaution when visiting a mother and new baby, lest bad luck come in with her.

Within the hut Nomusa saw many women assembled; she recognized Lutuli's wife immediately because she was smeared all over with red clay, and so was the baby.

Nomusa bowed and said, "My father, Chief Zitu, has sent me to ask if Buselapi is here. We need her."

"She was here, my child, until a short time before

you arrived. I shall send one of my older sons to run after her and bring her back before she reaches Umbumbulu," and he went outdoors.

Nomusa was invited to sit down and wait. They were getting ready to bathe the baby in a hole in the floor filled with warm water. As Nomusa watched, Lutuli's wife told her, "We have put a piece of *umalali* plant in the water to make the baby a quiet child."

Nomusa watched and listened carefully. *"Umama,"* called the baby's mother to the grandmother, "don't forget we have to strengthen the baby against dangers which may arise during the next few moons. Here are the powdered whiskers of a leopard, the skin of a salamander, and the claw of a lion to make him brave."

While these were being burned, the grandmother held the baby in the smoke, and the mother chanted the new lullaby she had composed especially for this child.

Lutuli re-entered the hut and said, "Your little brother has gone with my son to find Buselapi. Please make yourself at home."

The tiny baby was handed to his father who held him tenderly; then he passed him between his legs across

the smoke of the hearth to the mother. "This will prevent my son from becoming a lazy person," he said.

Nomusa nodded. Lutuli continued, "I know Buselapi thinks all this is nonsense, but one can't be sure. Our *idlozi* might be very displeased if we put aside all our old customs."

The friendliness of the group encouraged Nomusa to ask Lutuli's wife, "Was Buselapi helpful?"

"*Ayi!* What a question! She is an expert. Still, there are things in which I do not agree with her. She does not believe that I mustn't eat the meat of the hare in order that my baby not have long ears, and things like that."

Suddenly someone outside said, "Here she is!"

Buselapi entered anxiously. Nomusa jumped up and ran to her. "What's the matter, Nomusa?" she inquired.

"Mdingi! He's very sick. It began after the ear-piercing ceremony. The slits in his ears are full of evil spirits! We must go to him quickly or it will be too late," said Nomusa.

She looked down to see if Buselapi was carrying the bag which contained the magic medicine and was relieved to see she had it.

Buselapi asked, "Has anyone else been called in to help him?"

"Of course, the *inyanga* came," said Nomusa, "but this time the curse was too heavy, and she was not successful."

"Let's go to him at once, Nomusa. It sounds like blood-poisoning. I only hope I have enough penicillin."

They bowed and left Lutuli and his family. Themba

was waiting outside when they went past him, and he had to run to keep up with them.

Buselapi slowed down her pace and took Themba's hand. She told Nomusa, "Let's not walk so fast. A few moments more or less now won't make much difference in conquering Mdingi's germs, if his sickness is what I think it is. Only, I'm not sure I have enough penicillin with me. I had to use a good deal on Lutuli's wife."

Nomusa grew a little desperate at the thought of the insufficient supply of the magic medicine and said, "Mdingi is not the only one having trouble with his ear slits. Maboko has the same sickness. It will be bad without your medicine."

"Well, let's not worry until we get there," said Buselapi. "I wonder how all this happened? Probably the ear-piercing doctor's hands and knife had germs on them, and so they got into the ear slits. It is for this reason that I try so hard to teach our people to take care, and not blame everything on evil spirits, on the curse of an enemy or on the anger of their *idlozi*."

"Do you mean, Buselapi, that Mdingi's sickness could have come from the evil-spirit germs on the ear-piercing doctor's hands or knife?" Nomusa asked, brightening.

Themba watched Nomusa's change of mood and wondered why she should be so pleased when Mdingi was still in trouble and the magic medicine hadn't even been used yet.

Nomusa continued excitedly, "Buselapi, don't you think that if someone was at the *qhumbuza* who shouldn't have been there, our *idlozi* would certainly put a curse on some of the boys whose ears were pierced?"

"It would have nothing to do with it!" declared Buselapi. "The only thing that could cause the festering and put the germs into the blood would be either the unclean knife, or the dirty hand of the ear-piercing doctor, or both. By the way, was anyone else there who touched their ears?"

"I didn't see anyone excepting the ear-piercing doctor and the man who handed him the pieces of cornstalk to put in the slits," said Nomusa, not realizing she had given herself away.

"*Hau!*" gasped Themba in astonishment. "Then *you* were there, Nomusa! What will *Ubaba* say?"

$\mathcal{N}$OMUSA HID her face in her hands and burst
into tears, overcome with shame. She turned
away from Buselapi and Themba and ran
ahead sobbing.

Soon Buselapi ran after her. "Nomusa!" she
pleaded, putting her arms around her. "Wait and listen
to me, please. And you too, Themba. What happened

to Mdingi and Maboko has nothing whatever to do with whether you were at the ceremony or not. We Zulus have many beautiful and useful customs which help to keep us united and proud. But there are others that are no longer sensible. It is necessary to show respect for the ways and traditions of our people, and we should remember our *idlozi* and behave properly so they won't be ashamed of us, but now I have learned the real reason for many sicknesses."

Nomusa looked up, listening hard. Themba rushed up to her and took her hand. "It wasn't you, my sister, who caused the sickness," he echoed. "I'm certainly going to tell *Ubaba* about the germs on the ear-piercing doctor's knife and hands so he'll be punished!"

Buselapi smiled and said, "When we return to your father's kraal let's not talk about what we have been saying here. First I must try the penicillin, and if it works we'll not have to worry about what Chief Zitu will say about Nomusa watching the ceremony. Agreed?"

She was glad to see her companions more cheerful and now they walked together, lightheartedly discussing Lutuli's baby and the plans for Khotiza's wedding.

Nomusa stopped suddenly and said, "Buselapi, if you succeed in curing Mdingi and Damasi's brother with your magic medicine, I promise to go to school and become a nurse, like you."

"Oh, Nomusa, you mustn't make your promise depend on that. I might not have enough penicillin now, but that shouldn't discourage you from wanting to go to school. If you didn't become a nurse, you could be a teacher and open a whole new world to our children and their parents. There is so much they must learn about health, the way to grow crops more efficiently, better ways of caring for and feeding babies and small children."

"We are listening," said Nomusa and Themba.

"And," Buselapi continued, "our people must learn to live in a more sanitary way. Because they don't know anything about germs, they blame sickness on bad luck, on enemies or on the *idlozi*. At school you will learn ways of preventing sicknesses and curing them."

They now saw Kangata running down the path to meet them. "Hurry, hurry!" he urged. "Mdingi is out of his head and is shouting things we can't understand. The curse put upon him is very heavy, and maybe noth-

ing will help him now. *Ubaba* and *Ugogo* are in the hut
with *Umama* waiting for you."

Buselapi quickened her steps and followed him into
the kraal. Softly they entered Makanya's hut.

Without paying any attention to which was the
men's or women's side of the hut, Buselapi went directly
to Mdingi. He tossed and mumbled, his face contorted.
She opened her bag quickly and took out a clean white

cloth, spreading it on the mat next to him. She placed the glass tube with the needle on it, and then she took out the bottle containing the magic medicine. Nomusa saw that it was only half full.

"Come here, Nomusa. I need your help," said Buselapi. "Hold the bottle of penicillin while I examine Mdingi."

Buselapi put her hand on Mdingi's hot forehead and saw red streaks radiating from his ears into his cheeks. From her pocket Nomusa saw her take out something small and round, which had black marks on it and ticked.

The nurse held Mdingi's wrist with her left hand while she clasped the ticking object in her right, staring at it intently. Never had any of them seen or heard such a thing. What kind of peculiar magic was this, they wondered?

Buselapi put away the ticking object and bent over Mdingi, examining his festering ears. The swelling had not only gone into his cheeks but had puffed up his eyes, too. It looked bad.

Everyone watched Buselapi closely. There was no

chanting, clapping, dancing, drumming. The stillness seemed strange and unbearable. Never had they seen such quiet treatment. What would the ancestors think of this, and would they grow even more displeased than they were?

Buselapi took the bottle from Nomusa and filled the glass tube with the penicillin. Carefully she wiped off a place on Mdingi's hip and injected the magic medicine into him. The unexpected thrust of the needle startled him, and he winced.

Nomusa shut her eyes and clasped her hands tightly. Themba, beside himself with nervousness, called out, "It's all right, Mdingi; the penicillin fang will kill the germs that are poisoning you, and you'll get better."

"Hot water, Nomusa. I want to wash his ear lobes and open the sores so the pus will ooze out," said Buselapi.

Nomusa fetched the water and, filling a half gourd, handed it to her. Into this Buselapi poured some medicine, then with a wad of something white that looked to Nomusa like the wool on a lamb's back, she gently washed Mdingi's ears.

He lay still now, letting her do whatever she wished.

Buselapi turned to Zitu. *"Inkosi,* with your permission, I shall spend the night here. In a few hours I must put more penicillin into Mdingi, and I shall continue giving it to him regularly until late tomorrow. I shall have to send someone to Umbumbulu for more penicillin for Damasi's brother."

Now there was nothing more to do but sit and wait and wonder if the magic medicine would help Mdingi. Everyone was silent, some staring into the hearth fire, some at Mdingi.

Ugogo finally rose and said, "I'll go back to my hut now. Nomusa, I need water."

Nomusa took the empty jar and followed her out. Sisiwe came to her and asked, "What news, my sister?"

"Buselapi is giving him the magic medicine and staying overnight. I feel easier in my heart now that she is here, especially after what she told me was the reason for most sickness."

"Guess what, Nomusa. Khotiza's wedding day has finally been set. Sigazi's father agreed to give the twelve cows for her. If Mdingi and Maboko get well, the wedding will take place on the first day of the next full moon."

"That is good news!" exclaimed Nomusa. "I'm glad Khotiza's worth was properly recognized."

When Nomusa returned from the stream she saw Buselapi outdoors with Themba and Bala; Dube was in her arms. Buselapi said, "Mdingi is sleeping soundly now, and I think that soon his skin will grow cooler. I have made him drink a great deal of water to wash out the poisons in his body, and I have also bathed him with a soothing substance to make him more comfortable. But he won't take anything to eat yet.

"I think it will be better if we stay outdoors so Mdingi will be quiet and undisturbed. Your father has gone back to his hut."

She walked with Nomusa to *Ugogo's* hut to leave the water. Buselapi sat waiting and was soon surrounded by the little sisters and brothers in the kraal.

They were drawn to her by her kindly manner. They knew she had come to cure Mdingi's sickness, but they were puzzled by her appearance and whispered to one another, "See, she's not dressed like an *inyanga* at all; she hasn't even one gall bladder stuck in her hair."

"And why doesn't she wear the crossed goatskin strips on her chest, or any bead necklaces?" asked another.

"What kind of an *inyanga* can she be without a gnu-tail wand-stick or shield?" wondered a boy.

Buselapi saw their questioning glances and said, "When Nomusa comes out of *Ugogo's* hut, would you like me to tell you a story?"

She looked into their interested faces; the children

were impatient for her to begin. When Nomusa reappeared, Buselapi began. She spoke well, telling them the story of her life with as much gusto and liveliness as *Ugogo* told her fanciful tales.

The children were held spellbound. Never had they heard such wonderful things. She told them about schools, about little black marks that could be put down on paper and learned, so that they could hear stories with their eyes as well as with their ears. She told them about giant huts called hospitals, where sick people were taken care of by people called doctors and nurses.

"We are listening," said the children, anxious for her to continue, but she rose and said, "I must go to Mdingi. It is time to give him his medicine."

Nomusa found her mother sitting beside Mdingi, holding his hand in both of hers. He was now sleeping and breathing more easily, but his dark skin still had a red flush under it that showed he was feverish. She wondered if Buselapi had exaggerated the magical powers of the new medicine.

Buselapi again took out the small ticking object with the glass face and black dots on it. Again she held

Mdingi's wrist with one hand while she stared at the ticking object in the other.

She told Makanya, "Things are not yet as they should be. I shall give him another injection of penicillin now, and one before we go to sleep."

Makanya's face showed her continued anxiety and also her suspicion of Buselapi's strange methods. Nomusa was also feeling less confident about her.

Nomusa's mother went to stir the cook pot, and said to Buselapi, "You have learned to drive away the evil spirits, or whatever the white man calls them, in a very quiet way. Do you think it will work as well as the chanting, clapping and the other methods of our *inyangas?*"

"I think you will see by and by that my way will work better," Buselapi said reassuringly.

That night Nomusa fell asleep on the mat next to Buselapi, still worried about Mdingi and uncertain about the magic medicine in which she had believed so thoroughly. Mdingi had already had his last injection for the night, and she had noticed his lusterless eyes as they fed him a little porridge. He seemed puzzled by Buselapi, wondering what kind of a witch doctor she was.

Nomusa slept fitfully, her heart still heavy. Next morning, when she awoke, she found that Buselapi was already up. She looked across the hut to see how Mdingi was. What Nomusa saw made her leap from her mat. Mdingi was sitting up! And all by himself! There was a bright expression on his thin face as Buselapi, ever so carefully, washed his sore ears and face. Like a member of the family, she had even started the fire under the cook pot and the water kettle.

Nomusa came over to them and knelt in front of

Mdingi. His face spread into a happy smile, as if he had been away from his sister for a long time and was now delighted to see her again.

Buselapi told her, "See, Nomusa, this morning your brother is much better. The new medicine is conquering the germs, just as I said it would."

In a weak voice, Mdingi said, "I hope that some day, my sister, you will become as good an *inyanga* as Buselapi."

Nomusa put her arms around Mdingi and said, "How happy I am, my brother, to see you able to sit up by yourself again. Buselapi is not an *inyanga,* but a nurse. She has used a medicine on you that is a new kind of magic."

"Oh, it is not magic," corrected Buselapi. "It is something you will learn about and understand when you go to school."

While they were talking, Chief Zitu entered the hut.

"Yo!" he exclaimed, "What is this I see to gladden my eyes? Mdingi sits, smiles, speaks! Well, I see that the new medicine Buselapi brought has restored my son to me. My heart is very happy for this, and I will make

her a generous payment to show my appreciation. Buselapi may ask whatever she wishes.''

Makanya, Nomusa, Themba, Kangata, and Bala listened, smiling happily. They all waited to hear, eager to know what Buselapi would request.

When she hesitated, Zitu said, "Don't be afraid or bashful about making a large demand. I am prepared to meet it because of what you have done for Mdingi.''

"There is only one thing I wish, *inkosi*.''

"Tell me,'' urged Zitu.

Nomusa looked at Buselapi, wondering what great demand she would make of her father. Soon she heard her saying, "All I ask is that you permit Nomusa to go to school and become a nurse. She is an exceptionally clever, strong girl who will be a credit to our people. There is much that a nurse can do in our Zululand, not only to help the sick but to keep people healthy and teach them things they need to know.''

Nomusa flushed with pride at Buselapi's words of praise. What would her father say to such an unusual request? Perhaps her father would be angry and drive Buselapi away for daring to ask such a thing.

She felt a thick silence descend upon the hut, and she was suddenly afraid.

Zitu sat down beside Mdingi and put his hand on his shoulder lovingly. Then he turned to Makanya and said, "My wife, if you can spare Nomusa, I am willing for her to go to school, and later she can become a nurse."

Nomusa's mother answered, "Our daughter is a great help to me, my husband, but I would not keep her tied to me. If she becomes as useful as Buselapi, she will then be able to help many, not just her mother and family."

"And now, my daughter, would you like to go to school and become a nurse?" Zitu asked Nomusa in a solemn voice.

"Oh, yes, *Ubaba,* I would!" exclaimed Nomusa enthusiastically. She fixed her shining eyes on Buselapi and said, "If I become a nurse I do not think our *idlozi* would be displeased. Perhaps they would even be proud, glad that I could help to teach our people new things and new ways, without neglecting our old customs and traditions which are beautiful and mean so much to us."

"Well said, Nomusa!" congratulated Zitu.

He then turned to Buselapi. "Your wish is granted, and in addition you may have two goats of your own choosing."

"I give you many, many thanks, *inkosi,*" said Buselapi, overcome with happiness for Nomusa. "Now I must go to help Damasi's brother. Stay well and remain in peace."

"I will go with you, Buselapi," said Nomusa, and followed her out of the hut. Proudly she carried Buselapi's little black bag with the precious magic medicine on top of her head, the proper way.